CAPO

Chris Black

Copyright © 2025 by Chris Black
All rights reserved.

No part of this book may be reproduced, stored in a retrieval system, or transmitted in any form or by any means—electronic, mechanical, photocopy, recording, or otherwise—without the prior written permission of the author, except for brief quotations used in reviews or scholarly works.

This is a work of fiction. Names, characters, places, and incidents are either the product of the author's imagination or used fictitiously. Any resemblance to actual persons, living or dead, events, or locales is entirely coincidental.

ISBN: 978-1-0682082-0-1
Cover design: Ryan Duguid
Printed by Amazon KDP

First edition published in the United Kingdom by Black Arts Development, 2025

Acknowledgements

To Angie, for listening through the scrap metal and helping me spot the silver. Thank you for reminding me I wasn't failing, just forging.
To Mum, Dad, and Caroline, thank you for making me feel capable even when I wasn't sure. This exists because you always made space for it to.

To Laurence my editor, for seeing it, for staying with it, and for helping me become the writer this story needed.
To Baz, for the map, the sand, and the spark. You'll know what I mean.
To Dairmuid, for trusting the story before it had pages, and helping aim it at the screen.
To those who read it in rough seas, and still believed it would find its way to shore. You know who you are.
To Stephen, my Lynch to this madness. Thank you for seeing what this could be before most others did, and for giving it the scope and edge it needed.
To the cast and crew who came together for the *Capo* concept, for turning script into breath, and belief into motion. That day still feels like the moment it became real.
To Ryan, my cover artist, thank you for giving this book its first impression, and for doing it with such precision and style.
To Black Arts, for being the vessel this story needed, even before it knew what it was.
And to the reader, thank you for choosing this one. I hope you find something worth holding onto.

PROLOGUE

Morocco, One Year Earlier
Desert Sky – Night

Against the darkened sky, two Apache attack helicopters moved in silhouette against the dark desert landscape.

A voice over the radio, thick with urgency and tension. "Alpha Sixteen, you are ordered to turn back. This is an unauthorised use of British assets—"

The message was abruptly cut off. The lead helicopter surged forward, carrying a lone figure strapped to its wing, huddled against the whipping wind and downdraft.

His face set, rage holding him together. The hurt was fresh, but there was no room for it. The wolf insignia on his shoulder was worn, ragged—earned.

The second Apache followed, each wing bearing a figure clinging tight, mirroring the lead.

The helicopters pressed onward, aiming at a lone compound emerging in the vast stretch of desert.

The compound sprawled across a footprint the size of Hampden Park, over 76,000 square feet of concrete bleached pale by years of unforgiving sun. Watchtowers on each corner. Trucks parked in rows. A satellite dish big enough to talk to God. Barbed wire all around. Built like a prison, run like a fortress. Barracks. Cell blocks. Drug labs. Families packed into shipping containers, women and children with nowhere else to go. Gun nests on the perimeter. Mines buried in the sand. Funded by diamonds. Ruled by fear.

On the ground before the compound, chaos spread, swift and uncontainable, rippling outward like wildfire. An overturned Humvee marked the end of a shattered convoy. Survivors ran for cover.

Jonesy's voice came through the closed comms like a 1970s BBC newsreader but with a warm undercurrent beneath that crisp accent. It softened the command, made it linger.

"Capo, Wolves. Compound in range. Aggressive infiltration and fire suppression in thirty seconds."

Inside the upturned Humvee, an American operative, Kev, fought against his seatbelt, his breathing fraught and panicked.

Fuel dripped onto his face, mixing with the grit of sand as bullets thudded into the chassis. One finally shattered the passenger window. He barely registered the distant thunder of rotor blades, growing louder with each second.

"Fuck, fuck…" Kev's voice shook as he cursed himself.

Boots approached. Kev froze, eyes clamped shut as he braced for the inevitable. But the only sound that followed was the furious crescendo of helicopter rotors overhead and the monstrous bursts of an M230 Bushmaster cannon, lighting up the night in brutal, rapid fire. Empty cartridges clattered around him as the Apaches touched down in a whirlwind of sand, noses pitched high to continue the onslaught.

"Dismount," a voice commanded, steely and resolute.

Ezio Trevino unlatched his harness, rolling as he dropped backward off the Apache's wing onto the ground. Two Marines did the same nearby, moving in silent coordination. Ezio blinked hard, clearing sweat and the sting of tears from his vision. He scanned the ground. The helicopters lifted, kicking up clouds as the

Marines advanced, systematically cutting down the last of the resistance.

Ezio made for the wreckage. As bullets flew and flames crackled, the Wolves formed a protective ring around him, laying down covering fire. His rifle stowed, Ezio reached for his knife, his movement fluid and practised. Kev let out a strangled scream as the blade sliced through his seatbelt.

With a forceful tug, Ezio pulled Kev from the wreckage. "Move," he ordered, his voice cold and steady.

Kev staggered to his feet, propelled forward by Ezio's grip. The Marines fell back in sync, the four of them sprinting away from the Humvee. Just as they cleared it, a thunderous explosion rocked the night, flames erupting from the wreckage, searing against the cool desert air, the shockwave hurling the four across the sand.

CHAPTER 1

One Year Later

Glasgow, Present Day
Mullholland Bar – 23:30

Ezio Trevino's boots crunched against the frost-covered stone steps as he descended to Mullholland's entrance, his breath clouding in the bitter December air. Inside, the amber glow from a vintage ceiling lamp bathed Mullholland in warmth, where the faint clink of glasses blended into the stillness. Kev stowed freshly washed, still warm glasses under the bar.

Mullholland wasn't a large place. A narrow basement property wedged between a designer waxing salon on one side, and on the other, an upscale hotel with sleek glass panels, a concierge at the door, and a rooftop bar with skyline views.

You entered from the street, descending sixteen flagstone steps. Just inside, the long wooden bar stretched down the room along the wall to your left. On your immediate right, a small raised stage sat tucked in front of a floor-to-ceiling window that ran along the front wall. A decal of a howling wolf silhouetted inside a full moon was imposed on the glass.

The wall opposite the bar was lined with booths, and the main floor space was fitted with three high benches where you'd sit on stools to drink and banter.

Beyond the bar, a door led into Ezio's cramped office. Right of that, a short ramp ascended to a quieter nook with amber-lit booths that didn't come alive until around eleven on weekends. This was the area where Ezio was due to meet Morris Kingston this evening. By the end of the meeting, Mullholland would be electric.

Ezio tugged off his gloves, hung his long wool coat by the heater, and straightened. He scanned the room, his eyes lingering on the details—details he'd fought hard to bring to life.

Kev popped up from behind the bar, catching him mid-thought. "Yeah, I do that sometimes too, you know."

Ezio was quiet for a moment, then spoke, his voice low. "We've come a long way in one year."

"You're right to be proud of what you've done," said Kev.

Ezio snorted, but there was no humour in it. "At what cost?"

Kev rested an elbow on the bar, chin in hand. "Don't start with that, Mr Broody Capo Man. It is not just the bar, and you know it. You did not simply turn a shit-hole into the best place in town. You changed lives. Chris and Reddy are home. Annabelle's out of that mess she was in. And me…" He paused. "You gave me a shot. An American transgender spy, outcast by my own country and my so called family? I never thought I'd be safe, let alone have a home. But now I do. My wife and kid do."

Ezio moved to the bar, gesturing to the top shelf. "Macallan."

Kev grabbed the bottle of dark liquid and set it down beside a clean glass. "Here. Quit wallowing."

Ezio poured himself a measure, "Thanks."

Kev leaned in, "So, what's eating you?"

Ezio stared at the glass for a moment, then emptied it in one go. "We're close to locking down the package." He set the glass down with a solid thud. "He's meeting me in the back soon. I don't know, maybe that's it."

"Pre-game nerves? That's new," said Kev, eliciting a grunt from Ezio. "Annabelle's in the office, by the way. Says she's got a favour to ask."

Ezio sighed, pushing himself up with effort. "The joys. She knows we're skint. Hope she's not trying to empty my pockets."

Ezio nudged his office door ajar as Kev called after him. "Matter of the heart, I understand."

Inside Ezio's office, Annabelle was sprawled in Ezio's chair, stockinged feet kicked up on the desk like she owned the place. Her dark brown eyes bulged, her expression incredulous. "What did he just say?" she demanded.

Ezio stepped inside, closing the door behind himself. His hand moved smoothly to his belt, drawing a Colt 1911 from its concealed holster and stowing it in a filing cabinet. "Feet down. Out of my chair."

Annabelle scowled but didn't waste time. She spun out of the chair and shoved her toes into a pair of trainers. Her heels barely inside. Each step landed with a heavy clomp. "What did he say?" she demanded, crossing her arms tightly over her chest.

Ezio closed the cabinet door. "Didn't hear. Just said you wanted to speak to me."

She relaxed and perched her bum against the desk. But Ezio wasn't in the mood to indulge. "Before you start," he said, cutting her off before she could open her mouth. "Two things. First, we're skint. You know this already. Second, I've got a meeting, any moment now. So whatever this is, make it quick."

Annabelle clapped her hands like a demented seal. "Oh, is it Marty?"

"What? No, it's not Marty." Ezio stopped, narrowing his eyes at her. "Actually, he might be there. You're driving at something. What's your angle?"

Annabelle straightened. "Driving. Yes, I like your train of thought. I understand a road trip might be in the works, and I thought maybe…?"

"No," said Ezio.

"Why not?" said Annabelle.

"Because it's too dangerous. I'm not risking your life or everything we've built just so you can drool over your crush. Any more questions?"

Annabelle pouted, arms crossed. "You're so unreasonable."

"Yes, I am," he said.

Ezio stepped back into the bar, Annabelle trailing behind. She shuffled her feet as her sulk carried her behind the bar and into the kitchen.

Chris, caught mid-pour, froze like a child caught stealing sweeties. "I was just testing the keg," he said, lifting the pint defensively.

"Hey, it's your bar too. You don't have to explain to me. Where's Kev?" asked Ezio.

Chris sipped his pint. "Downstairs. I sent him to change the keg. That's a Kev job, not a Chris job," he said, tilting his head toward the tap. "You want one?"

"No thanks. Morris will be here any minute," said Ezio.

"The shipment?" asked Chris.

"I hope so. But you never can tell," Ezio replied.

Chris snorted. "Old bastard. Bet he'll try getting under your skin before sliding it in there."

"You can count on that," Ezio said.

Just then, Reddy stomped into the room, his boots thumping on the wheelchair access ramp to the back area. A whirlwind of energy and bad timing. Reddy held an assortment of coloured pencils and sheets of A4 paper, his grin broad as he thrust one sheet in Ezio's face. "Cracked it?" Reddy announced.

"Cracked what?" said Ezio.

Reddy waved the paper. "In case we have to hit a first-floor warehouse. I've drawn up a unique yet cost-effective solution for infiltration."

Ezio took the paper cautiously. "Did you draw a fire engine?"

"Yeah, with toboggans!" said Reddy.

Chris leaned in. "Where's the firemen?"

Reddy scoffed. "We're the firemen. Anyway, this isn't for you." He turned back to Ezio. "What do you reckon, Cap?"

Ezio handed the paper to Chris. "It's, uh, really inventive, mate. Tell you what, let Chris pour you a pint, and we'll chat about it after I meet with Morris. Fresh keg."

Reddy slapped Ezio on the back, hard enough to jolt him forward. "Good plan, boss! Can't decide anything important with a clear head. Otherwise, we'd never get anything done," he said, stomping off toward the bar with a maniacal cackle.

Ezio and Chris exchanged looks. "I'll be in the back," Ezio said, moving toward the corridor.

"Cool, I'll round up the others and have a cold one waiting for you," said Chris.

"Thanks, mate," said Ezio as he turned down the short corridor. He stepped into the rear room and slid into a booth facing the door. Spotting a sheet of paper, loose from a stack Reddy had likely left behind, he folded it into an aeroplane, his gaze drifting briefly to the door.

Back in the main bar, Annabelle and Kev reappeared from the kitchen. Reddy stood animated, taking the floor with an exaggerated stance as he launched into a story, half-myth, half-memory, voice carrying over the quiet of the room. "I called it the rise and die," he said. "I invented it myself. Stopped Jonah Lomu dead in his tracks with it."

Chris shook his head. "No, you didn't, mate."

Annabelle shot Chris a look.

Chris raised his hands in surrender. "Hey, it's you that has to listen to this fable," he said.

Annabelle turned back to Reddy whose eyes were wild. "So there we were, two monsters in our prime. I spotted him in the tunnel. He knew it. He knew I was dangerous, I tell you. He knew."

Annabelle laughed, tucking her hair behind her ear. "So how do I do it?" she asked, adopting a wide stance and tugging her jeans up, mimicking Reddy's posture.

Reddy nodded approvingly, their eyes locked, intense. "You have to anticipate their run, watch how they move," he coached, "and when they come close, you catch them high, wrap your arms, and push up from your arse as hard as you can."

The group's laughter spilled into the hall, carrying toward the back area where Ezio waited, his gaze sharp, face expressionless.

The door to the back room creaked open. Morris Kingston entered, his eyes cold and calculating. Morris was followed closely by Marty and Eammon. Eammon slid into the booth across from Ezio, while Marty lingered near the door.

Morris had once been more than this a mentor, friend to Ezio's father, and a man he trusted. Back then, before his dad's death and before the Marines, Morris was like an uncle. Now he ran Glasgow, and whatever they'd once been to each other didn't seem to count for much.

Morris eyed Ezio, who barely looked up, focused on folding paper planes. "Making paper planes, son?" Morris's voice dripping with disdain.

He looked around and spotted a tray perched on the piano at the other side of the room, on it a couple of short glasses and a bottle of whisky.

Morris watched Ezio for any reaction as he carried the glasses and the bottle over to Ezio's table, slapped them noisily on the table's surface. Morris poured as he smiled with menace, his gaze lingered on Ezio. Who, though outwardly calm, simmered inside. "Is that what you did over there? Made paper planes for the babies… after you shot their daddies?"

Ezio remained silent, hands working the paper in steady, mechanical motions.

Morris smirked as he settled into the booth. "You've done well with your little misfits," he sneered, nodding toward the noise coming from the front.

Through the booth window, Annabelle playfully tackled Reddy, causing a loud thump and commotion as Chris and Kev rushed to help their friends from the floor. Reddy cried out grumbling as they descended into laughter.

"But don't you forget," Morris leaned in, his voice low, "you've got nothing. You work for me."

Ezio's jaw tightened, his voice cold and clipped. "The job's getting done. You needed a captain. You got one."

Morris smirked, tilted his glass. "Oh, sure," he said, mockingly. "But remember the rules, Captain Trevino… or should I say, *The Wolf*?" He let the insult linger, his gaze hardening. "If your daddy could see you now. Nice car, fine suit, and scrabbling for every penny."

Morris noticed the scene beyond the booth window and muttered to himself, "Smiling faces, but none for me…" Returning his attention to Ezio, he added, "Who was it that took you in after you boys got back?" His stare pinned Ezio, that dangerous edge creeping in.

"If you're unhappy with the job we're doing…" Ezio began.

"Oh, no. That's not what I'm saying," Morris interrupted, smirking as he held up a finger. "Boy who flew too close to the sun?"

Ezio didn't blink. "Icarus."

Morris nodded to himself, rolling one of Ezio's paper planes between his fingers. "Well, I'm the fucking sun."

He held it there, square in their line of sight, watching it burn before letting it drop onto the table.

Marty appeared next to them and slid a phone across the table, stopping it at Morris's fingertips. "Sir, your daughter."

Morris took the phone, still staring at Ezio. "Got a job for you," he said, smirking. He barely looked at Marty. "He'll fill you in." He stood, arms loose at his sides. Marty stepped in, helping him into his coat. Morris let it happen, slow, deliberate. Then, with a final mocking smile— "And do give your mother my best."

Just then, Annabelle burst through the door, breathless. She skidded to a stop, taking in Morris's menacing figure. "Ezio— oh, sorry, hi!"

Ezio shifted, quick and deliberate, slotting himself between Annabelle and Morris. "I'll be there in a second," he said, steady, his eyes still on Morris.

Annabelle hesitated, then backed out, glancing nervously at Morris.

Morris's eyes tracked her as he leered slyly. "Pretty," he murmured as he left, cruel satisfaction in his voice. Eammon hot on his heels like a puppy eager for scraps.

Marty waited for the door to click closed and stepped closer to Ezio, his expression grim. "Simple pickup job. No real risk, just the gun shipment from last year." He checked warily over his shoulder to be certain Morris had left and dropped his voice as he leaned in. "He's suspicious. Reckons selling you this place was a favour and you still owe him."

Ezio scoffed. "It was a run-down wreck and he charged me twice the going rate."

Marty nodded, barely a hint of sympathy in his face. "I know. Just play it smart," he said. "Everyone answers to someone, even Morris. Watch your back."

Ezio frowned, sensing the tension in Marty's tone. "Relax, Buttons."

"What?" Marty bristled but immediately shrugged it off. "Never mind," he muttered, leaving

Annabelle rushed back into the room, skidding to stop next to Ezio once more. "Bye, Marty!" she cooed, then nudged Ezio. "Well?"

Ezio grinned, teasing. "'Bye, Marty?'"

Annabelle punched his shoulder with a laugh. "Shut up! We just finished stock take. One for the road?"

"Is it ever just one?" said Ezio.

With her arm around his waist, Annabelle steered him back into the main room, where the others waited. Reddy handed Ezio a pint, clinking it with his own.

"You okay?" Chris asked, looking Ezio up and down.

"As much as I can be. Just another job, I suppose," Ezio replied, taking a sip.

"Not just any job," Reddy cut in, leaning closer. "This is the one. If we don't get to this shipment before the Semenov's, they'll kill us all and take this place without a second thought, then probably turn it into some seedy strip bar. Not to mention your mother. Chiara's medical bills? If you leave her in the hands of the NHS, she won't make the year, mate. But the package, the one ray of light to come out of that last fucking mission. Ezio, that package you hid with the guns that solves everything."

Chris nodded thoughtfully. "It's been over a year since we set this up. Everything else barely keeps us afloat. We don't get that package, we're ruined and exposed."

Reddy looked around at the others. "Get the package, clear the mortgage for this place, pay for your mum's treatment, and finally be rid of Morris," he said, his tone hopeful.

"That simple, huh?" Annabelle said.

"If only," Ezio muttered. "Apparently, I'm Icarus, and he's the sun."

Chris scoffed, shaking his head. "Mad bastard. Think he suspects?"

Ezio took a sip, catching the froth on his lip before swiping it away with his thumb. "Hard to say."

Reddy grinned. "Relax, you'll figure it out. You always do." He knocked his glass against Ezio's. "But for now, let's get pissed!"

Glasgow, the Following Day
Mullholland Bar – Afternoon

Later the following afternoon, Reddy squinted, his head throbbing. He winced as he poured lemonade into a pint glass, then topped it off with lager.

Two paracetamol went down with a grimace and a large gulp of shandy. Kev leaned against the bar, scrolling through his phone, but Reddy's pounding head barely registered his presence until Chris entered, looking fresh and chipper.

Chris smirked at Kev. "Ready for poetry night, Mr Compere? Rum and cake, a theme that might even tempt me."

Reddy's groggy eyes snapped toward Chris. "Wait, only rum?"

Kev, distracted by his checklist, didn't notice as Reddy stealthily stashed a bottle of rum behind the bar, grumbling under his breath, "It's my rum."

"Whatever," Kev replied absently, eyeing his list. "Did you order the cake?"

Reddy's guilty silence was answer enough. He squirmed, groaning, and Chris and Kev exchanged knowing looks just as Annabelle walked in, catching the end of their conversation. Her eyes widened as she pieced together what had, or hadn't, happened.

Annabelle snapped her fingers toward the door. "Well? Get over there now!"

She strode toward Reddy, who, realising he had no way out, gulped down his shandy as fast as he could while Chris herded him toward the door.

Chris gave Kev a wink. "Don't worry. I've got you."

"My guy," said Kev.

Reddy and Chris stepped out through the door. As it swung shut, Annabelle slipped behind the bar, snatching up Kev's checklist. She leaned against the counter, her eyes scanning the list as Kev resumed scrolling on his phone. She sighed, more to herself than to anyone else. "Where's Ezio when you actually need him?"

"Taking his mother to the hospital," Kev said.

"That's tough," Annabelle mused, her tone soft.

"Yeah," Kev said, half-engaged, half-distracted by his phone. "He sees it as penance. Doesn't want to be disturbed. I've kept my texts to a minimum." Kev tapped out a quick message.

"At least he's trying," Annabelle said. "She's always on me to get him to visit."

"You two are close," Kev said, glancing up.

"Helping her at the soup kitchen brings me peace," said Annabelle. "I was in need

25

once, like those people. It does the soul good to give back, though that kitchen is the fanciest I've ever seen. Makes you wonder where the funds come from."

Kev laughed. "Yeah, don't. Personally, I'm just grateful for flamboyance."

Annabelle sighed. "I hope it is good news. I worry about her."

Kev set his phone down. "I worry about him."

Glasgow, Present Day
Our Lady in Chains Church – Afternoon

Across the city from Mullholland, outside Our Lady in Chains, Ezio shut the door of his Aston Martin Vantage, admiring the sleek lines of the new car. Adjusting his collar in the reflection, he took a breath before moving. His boots tapped lightly against the pavement as he passed a group of elderly parishioners filing onto a battered bus, bound for the hospital.

From across the churchyard, Chiara spotted him and hurried over, her arms outstretched. "Oh, my boy! I didn't think you'd remember. I was nearly on the bus."

Ezio met her halfway with a faint smile. "Never one to let a pretty lady down."

She snorted. "Always the charmer."

A heavy hand clamped Ezio's shoulder. He turned. Father McGrintle towered over him, smiling wide.

"Well, what a lovely surprise," McGrintle said. "How are you, my boy?"

"Good." Ezio barely nodded, turning to his mother. "Ma, let's go."

"Ezio Trevino! Don't be rude," Chiara chided.

McGrintle waved it off. "Not at all, Chiara. I just wanted to thank our generous benefactor. That soup kitchen, it's more like a bistro now."

Ezio's mouth twitched, humourless. "It's nothing." He gestured to his mother. "Ma."

Chiara shot the priest an apologetic smile. "Really, Father, I'm sorry." She turned to her son, wagging a finger. "And you better not drive too fast. You know I hate those race cars of yours."

Ezio raised an eyebrow. "Good thing I brought the company car."

"Company car!" Chiara scoffed. "Since when does a barman get a company car?"

Ezio opened his mouth to respond instantly but stopped himself. His phone buzzed. Ezio swiped it silent without checking the notifications and shoved it back into his pocket.

"I'd be fine on the bus, you know," she said. "I don't like all those bumps when you speed."

Ezio said nothing. McGrintle's fond gaze lingered. Ezio forced himself not to scowl. Instead, he gently offered his mother his arm, helped her into the car, shut the door behind her. When he glanced back, McGrintle stood on the steps, hands clasped as he watched them go.

Ezio slid into the driver's seat, started the engine, and pulled away without looking back.

Glasgow, Present Day
Mullholland Bar – Afternoon

Inside Mullholland, Kev leaned against the bar, arms folded, watching Annabelle stretch precariously for the top shelf from a small stepladder.

"Kev, have you seen that dark rum? The Rumajola," she asked, fingers brushing bottles.

"Third one along," Kev said. "I remember replacing it."

Annabelle felt along the row, her balance shifting. Kev smirked, patted his pockets, then pulled out his phone.

"Oh no, wait—"

Glasgow, Present Day
M8 Motorway – Afternoon

The Aston Martin's engine purred as Ezio drove. Chiara sat beside him, her gaze fixed forward.

"Don't you think you should thank him for all he does?" she asked.

"I pay for the whole thing, Ma," Ezio said, voice edged with frustration.

"Money isn't always the answer, Ezio."

"In this case, it helps."

"He does all the graft—you know, all that herding people around."

Ezio muttered under his breath, "He's done plenty."

"What was that?" she asked.

"Ma," Ezio said, louder, "where else do people eat bruschetta at a soup kitchen? Croque-monsieur? There isn't even soup!"

"You can't buy away everything," Chiara said softly.

"Most things," he retorted.

She was quiet for a moment. "Not a brain tumour."

The words cut hit him hard and Ezio's grip tightened on the wheel. He exhaled slow, reached for the stereo, and let an old song seep into the silence. They stared ahead.

"We can try," he whispered, almost to himself.

The chorus swelled, filling the car.

Chiara continued to stare ahead, eyes misted, then slowly her hand drifted to his on the gear stick, fingers trembling.

"Oh, Tommy, my dear Tommy," she murmured, voice distant. "Can we go to the pictures tonight in your new car?"

Ezio's chest tightened. He knew instantly that she wasn't speaking to him.

"Anything for my girl," he said, steadying his voice, swallowing the lump in his throat.

Chiara smiled, content, as she sank back into her seat.

Ezio steered the Aston onto the exit slip, easing into the Queen Elizabeth University Hospital car park. He pulled up further back than usual—less chance of some careless idiot swinging a door into his.

He killed the engine, stepped out, and moved around to open the door for his mother.

Chiara stepped out, smoothing down her coat. "Thank you, son," she said, her voice quieter now.

Ezio exhaled, rolled his shoulders, the stiffness loosening. He started to speak, but a low thump carried through the air, distant at first, then building.

A bright yellow helicopter roared in, dominating the sky as it banked toward the hospital rooftop ahead. Ezio's gaze locked onto it, the sound pressing down on him, relentless. "Always," he murmured. "You know I'm always here for…" His voice faded as the aircraft disappeared beyond the top of the building.

Chiara tilted her head, eyes narrowing. "Yes?" she prompted gently.

Ezio blinked, "What?"

"Always here for…?"

He didn't respond.

Chiara huffed. "Forget it," she said, striding ahead.

Moroccan Desert, One Year Earlier
Inside a Known Terrorist Compound Near Tangier – Night

The air reeked of burning fuel, thick and bitter, but Ezio barely noticed. The heat, the dust, the gunfire—it all blurred into the chaos hammering through his skull. He pushed forward, shaking off Reddy's grip, ignoring Chris's pull at his arm.

"Inaya!" His voice ripped through the night, ragged, desperate.

She was there, sprawled on the floor. She was trapped, bleeding out. Firelight danced across her face—still beautiful, even now. Her deep blue eyes locked onto his, glassy with pain.

Chris hauled at Ezio's body armour, straining to pull him back. "Ezio, you're gonna get yourself killed!"

"I don't care!" His voice cracked. He strained, gaining a forward step. "She's pregnant! I love her, our fucking child!"

Reddy and Chris faltered, their grip loosening in that moment. Ezio lurched forward, reaching—closer now.

"Inaya, stay with me!"

Her lips moved as she whispered something he couldn't hear over the roar of the chopper, the gunfire splitting the night. Then her head tipped sideways. The light in her eyes dimmed.

Ezio dropped to his knees. Heat licked at his skin, but he didn't feel it. He reached out, fingers trembling, useless.

"No!"

A scream tore through him, raw, hopeless.

Reddy hauled him back, his grip monstrous. "She's gone! There's nothing you can do!"

Ezio turned, ready to swing, to fight. His fists curled, but the strength wasn't there. His chest heaved, the breath ripped from him in broken gasps.

Chris gritted his teeth and hauled him up. "Sorry, mate. We've got to go."

His legs buckled. Reddy and Chris didn't let him fall. They dragged him toward the extraction point as the fire swallowed what was left of his world.

The rotors pounded overhead. Gunfire spat through the dark.

Ezio didn't hear any of it.

All he heard was her voice.

And all he saw were those blue eyes. Gone.

Glasgow, Present Day
Queen Elizabeth University Hospital Car Park – Afternoon

Ezio stood frozen. His eyes fixed on the ground, unmoving.

Chiara had walked ahead, but when she turned, she found him still standing there, pale. "Ezio?"

Nothing.

She took a step closer. "Ezio?"

A blink. Like surfacing from deep water. But his eyes were wrong—flat, distant.

She'd never seen him like this. Not as a man. Not even as a boy.

Ezio's shoulders dropped as he finally moved, slow, deliberate. His lips barely parted, but she caught it.

"Sorry—"

Chiara hooked her arm through his, firm but gentle. "It's okay, son. We can do this."

He felt her touch before he saw it. He paused, then looked to her hand on his arm. He placed his hand over hers.

They walked through the hospital doors together.

Glasgow, Present Day
Queen Elizabeth University Hospital Heli-Deck – Afternoon

The pilots stepped off the helideck ramp, the steady hum of the hospital swallowing them. A patient, their passenger minutes ago, was wheeled past with haste.

Jonesy watched them go. She tugged at her jumpsuit collar, letting out the heat trapped against her skin.

Beside her, Tom made a weird little choking noise.

She turned. His face was pink.

"Something in your throat, Tom?"

"Nah, I'm good," he croaked.

"Relax," she said, still amused.

The lad was green, fresh out of flight school, but better than most. He didn't swagger. Didn't try to impress her. That counted for something.

Tom checked his watch, then shot her a sheepish look. "I'm starving. Coffee and cake downstairs?"

"Why not? I'm dying for a piss." She was already moving.

Tom hesitated, then fell in step. He'd learn to keep up.

Glasgow, Present Day
Queen Elizabeth University Hospital
Waiting Area – Afternoon

Ezio dropped his coffee cup into the bin and stepped into the waiting area, head down, swiping away another message from Kev.

Too late, he looked up.

He walked straight into someone stepping out of the restroom.

"Sorry!" Ezio looked up, grinned, caught off guard.

A short pilot, flight suit snug, patches giving her away instantly.

"Jonesy?"

"Capo?" Same disbelief.

They froze. A thousand unsaid things passed between them before a voice cut through the corridor.

"Jonesy! Emergency call!"

She snapped a look down the hall, then back to Ezio. Torn.

"Good to see you," she said, already stepping away. A quick, genuine smile. "I owe you a pint."

Ezio nodded. "Go."

She shot him one last look before disappearing toward her waiting co-pilot, Tom holding the key to the express elevator. Ezio watched her go, barely believing the coincidence.

His back ached as he dropped into a chair. The consultant doctor was already approaching, soft-soled shoes whispering against the floor.

"Mr Trevino?"

Ezio looked up. "Doctor?"

She sat beside him. "Your mother's tough. We'll need to adjust her treatment, but bringing her here saved her life."

Ezio exhaled. "Thank you, doctor."

"Still a road ahead, but she's in good hands now."

He nodded. The consultant was already moving, crossing the room to another waiting relative.

A young woman, mid-twenties, poor thing, stiff as stone. The doctor's voice carried. "Mrs Riley, I'm sorry. Your son—" The rest faded.

She sobbed.

Ezio turned away. His chest tightened again, but he shoved it down.

Chiara appeared, quiet, steady. She took in the scene, then slipped her arm through his.

Ezio glanced at her, squeezed her hand.

They left without a word, walking in step.

Glasgow, Present Day
Mullholland Bar – Afternoon

Mullholland was quiet. Annabelle and Kev clinked glasses, sipping banana daiquiris made with Reddy's hoarded Rumajola Jamaican rum.

"Mission accomplished," Kev said, tipping his glass toward the dark bottle on the counter. "I knew that scoundrel had it tucked away."

Annabelle raised her glass. "Should've been a detective." She took a slow sip, peering at him over the rim.

Kev grinned. "Layers, Annabelle. Depths."

She snorted, then choked as the daiquiri shot up her nose.

"Smooth," Kev said.

"Shut up," she spluttered, laughing.

Their laughter swelled, loose and easy.

Then— *bang*.

The door bursting open, slamming against the wall. The sound hit like a gunshot.

They froze, laughter cut dead.

Glasgow, Present Day
Queen Elizabeth University Hospital Car Park – Afternoon

Ezio slid into the driver's seat, the Aston's memory settings adjusting the vehicle around him. Chiara shut her door just as the hands-free lit up. Kev.

Ezio exhaled.

"Take it," Chiara said, nudging him.

He groaned but hit the button. "Kev, I left clear instructions not to be…"

"Boss, it's Annabelle," Kev snapped. "She's gone. That Albanian guy."

Ezio's grip tightened on the wheel. "Gone?" His voice cooled. "What do you mean, gone? Like on a date? That's not my problem, is it?"

Chiara smacked his hand, light but firm. "Be nice."

"Hi, Ma," Kev shot back. "No, like kidnapped. For real."

Ezio closed his eyes, fingers pressing his temple. Chiara sat up straighter, her smile gone.

He gritted his teeth. "Alright. I'm on my way."

The engine roared, tyres bit into asphalt as Ezio sped them off, back toward the looming city.

CHAPTER 2

Glasgow, Present Day
Gina Kingston's Office – Afternoon

Gina scowled at her phone. Call dropped again.

"Dad," she muttered, tossing it aside.

She grabbed her jacket. Slipped cash, a USB stick, and a switch-knife into her clutch. Her eyes caught on the open drawer. The bag of white powder. The platinum pipe.

The door creaked.

Skip hovered in the entrance, eyes wary. "Morris?"

"He's not picking up. I'm going over." She strode toward him, waving him off. "Shoo."

Skip scurried out of the office. The door clicked shut behind him.

Gina reached the door, hesitated. Fingers still on the handle.

She turned. Looked at the drawer again.

"Why not?" she murmured.

The drawer slid open. A line of powder vanished.

Glasgow, Present Day
Full Crumb Bakes, Victoria Road –
Afternoon

Jackie dusted icing sugar into a bowl, the fine white powder swirling. Reddy's gaze shifted between the sugar and the cakes behind the glass.

"Dark chocolate and Jammie Dodger," he breathed.

Chris leaned against the counter, unimpressed. "Aye?"

Reddy crouched, face near-pressed to the glass. Too close. His wide-rimmed cowboy hat tapped the display, and before he could adjust, he lost his balance, landing flat on his arse. "It's witchcraft."

Chris shook his head, barely sparing him a glance. He turned back to Jackie. "So yes, to answer your question. Kate's playing at Mullholland next week."

Jackie's fingers drummed against the counter, her face brightening. "So my intuition was right? She must be going places if she's playing at The Wolf."

Chris frowned. "Who calls it that?"

"Nobody I know," Jackie said, grinning.

Before Chris could respond, Reddy spun on him, so close Chris caught the full blast of Rumajola on his breath, which reeked of burnt sugar and bad decisions.

"No Cherry Oreo Chip. I'm concerned. What do we do?" he whispered, loudly.

Chris, determined not to encourage Reddy, did his best to ignore the man's theatrics. "Kate's doing great. Even Ezio's thrilled. He reckons we got her at just the right time."

Glasgow, Present Day
Victoria Road – Afternoon

Gina Kingston strode down Victoria Road with purpose, heels clicking a rhythm against the pavement. Ahead, two tracksuit lads with greedy grins loitered at the corner, beady eyes locked on the pink clutch in her grip.

One stepped forward, snarling. "That's a pretty wee pink pocket, darling."

Gina stopped. She shifted her hips, a slow, deliberate movement. Her fingers dipped into the clutch. Nothing in her face suggested fear. Nothing suggested anything at all.

She opened the bag, smiling. The lads' grins widened. An easy mark.

"It is tiny," she said.

Gina tilted her head forward, raised her eyes to them and purred. "Very tight indeed." Then quipped, "Still, it's a pocket neither of you little boys could ever hope to fill." She blew them a kiss.

Their grins vanished. One of the lads stepped closer. "Dirty bitch," he spat. "Maybe that's no' all we take aff ye."

Gina rolled her eyes. She didn't answer. The switch-knife snapped open, catching a glint of sunlight. She shifted her weight again, solid on her heels. Eyes on them. Waiting.

Glasgow, Present Day
Full Crumb Bakes, Victoria Road –
Afternoon

Jackie placed one of her famous Full Circle boxes on the counter alongside the others with a flourish. "There you are. A Muffin selection box and three cookie mix boxes, all our newest, tastiest treats."

Reddy spun around, his excitement bubbling over for what felt like the umpteenth time. "Cherry Oreo Chip?"

Chris let out a slow breath, "It's just the new stuff, mate."

Undeterred, Reddy leaned in close, his voice dropping to a conspiratorial whisper. "Chris, I need Cherry Oreo Chip. It is very important to me."

Chris shot him a sceptical glare but didn't have time to respond. A sharp scream carried in from outside. A man's scream. Jackie's head snapped toward the window, drawing Chris's attention.

"Is that…" he started.

Jackie's eyes widened. "Holy fuck."

Reddy, still upset that his cookie dilemma wasn't being taken seriously, looked between the pair, confused. "What?" he demanded, reluctantly turning to follow their gaze.

Glasgow, Present Day
Victoria Road – Afternoon

The teens stumbled back, scuffed and shaken. One rubbed his arm, eyes darting to the shop window. The other's head jerked up, following his mate's wide-eyed stare. Inside, Jackie, Chris, and Reddy stared back. Shocked.

Reddy's glare burned through the glass.

"Is that…a cowboy hat?" one muttered, squinting as if his eyes deceived him.

The second didn't answer. Gina skipped a step forward.

"Run!" screamed the other.

They bolted, tripping over each other, sprinting like hellhounds were on their heels.

Gina watched, unfazed. She turned, catching and admiring her own reflection in the glass, then the faces beyond it—Chris, open-mouthed. Jackie, blinking. Reddy, head tilted, furious and still.

She snapped the knife shut, dropped it into her clutch as if it were a tube of lipstick. Then grinned.

"Hi, boys!" she cooed, throwing them a little wave before strutting off, her hips swaying like she owned the ground she walked on, her heels clicking like punctuation against the pavement.

Glasgow, Present Day
Full Crumb Bakes, Victoria Road –
Afternoon

Reddy turned to Chris, head cocked, all spaniel-like confusion. "Gina fucking Kingston, eh?"

Chris exhaled, rubbing his jaw, finding a grain of sympathy within himself as he glanced toward Jackie. "Could you add a couple of Cherry Oreo Chip, please, pal?"

Glasgow, Present Day
Mullholland Bar – Afternoon

Kev surveyed the wreckage around him, running a hand through his hair as he took in the smashed glasses and overturned stools. He poured himself a stiff drink, took a deep sip, and let his gaze drift absently to his phone. A voice crackled from the speaker, startling him.

"Kev?"

Shock rolled into relief, sudden and overwhelming. Kev let out a long breath. "Yeah, I'm here."

"We're pulling back into the city," Ezio continued. "Did you see them leave?"

Kev nodded out of habit, mind racing. "I did. They didn't even bother hiding their faces."

Glasgow, Present Day
City Centre Streets – Afternoon

Ezio focused on the road. Chiara sitting beside him, her eyes sharp with concern.

"Black BMW 5 series," Kev's voice filtered through the speakers. "Plates HK19 IMO, blacked-out windows. Guy's been around, saying he wants to take Annie back to Lithuania for a 'better life'. Whatever that means."

Chiara threw her hands up, exasperated. Ezio exhaled. "Kev, why would an Albanian take her to Lithuania?"

A moment of silence before Kev replied, sheepish. "Isn't that where they're from?"

Chiara bit back a laugh.

Ezio's voice came dry. "No."

Kev tried again. "Extradition?"

"Extra-*what*?"

"Luther said it once," Kev added.

"Whatever. Can you track Annabelle's phone?"

"She dropped it," Kev replied. "It's still here."

Ezio pulled up at a red light. He scanned the passing traffic. A black BMW suddenly tore through the intersection, narrowly missing other cars. Ezio muttered, "HK19 IMO."

He and Chiara exchanged a quick, astonished look.

"Get after them!" she urged.

Kev's voice crackled through the speakers, confused. "Get after what now?"

Ezio stamped on the accelerator. The rear wheels skidded, tyres shrieking as the car ripped through the red light. "Kev, we've got them. I'm following."

"Wait, how?" Kev asked, bewildered.

"Doesn't matter. Patch in Chris and Reddy."

The BMW raced ahead, cutting through traffic. Ezio kept his grip loose, letting the car glide into the chase. Onlookers flinched as the Aston skidded through a tight turn, the engine growling as he steadied the wheel. He didn't need to push it—just keep them in sight. The BMW weaved. Ezio matched them, patient.

The BMW's driver glanced into his rear-view mirror, expression shifting to a knowing smile as he recognized the unmistakable silhouette of Ezio Trevino's Aston Martin.

Glasgow, Present Day
Victoria Road – Afternoon

Reddy and Chris strolled down the street toward Reddy's SUV. Chris carried a bag full of cake boxes, shifted it from one hand to the other. Reddy inspected his own singular box, nose deep like a man hypnotised.

"Mission successful," Chris muttered, shifting the bag again.

"Yeah, but Gina Kingston—that was wild," Reddy mumbled into his cake box. He didn't look up. "Chris? You're sure you got it?" he whined.

Chris shot him an exasperated look. Reddy's big head emerged from the box, his expression sheepish, and immediately shrank back. He pulled his key fob from his pocket with a nervous smile. "Maybe I can wait till we get back…"

Before Chris could reply, Reddy's phone abruptly blared to life with the shrill, breathy notes of a pan flute. Reddy froze, still clutching the cake box in one hand and the key fob in the other. His eyes darted helplessly to Chris.

Shakira's voice erupted: *"Whenever, wherever…"*

Chris sighed. "Just put it back in your pocket."

Reddy glanced between the cake box and the key fob in confusion, Shakira's warbling growing louder. Chris rolled his eyes. "No—put the key fob… Oh, fine, come here."

Chris reached over and yanked the phone from the back pocket of Reddy's ridiculous shorts. He swiped the screen, silencing Shakira, and quickly put the call on speaker.

Kev's unmistakable Californian accent punched through, urgent and strained, "Oh, thank God."

Chris and Reddy exchanged wary looks. "Everything's fine, Kev," Chris said cautiously. "We got four boxes. Plenty for your poetophiles. You got the rum?"

"Forget that!" Kev snapped. "Annabelle's been taken, and we need you."

Reddy and Chris froze, their eyes wide.

Ezio's voice cut in, smooth, unbothered. "Lads, don't let him panic you. I'm in pursuit—I've got it handled."

The pair stood in the middle of the street. Chris blinked. Reddy frowned. Flabbergasted, neither quite sure what to make of it.

"Annabelle's been taken?" Reddy repeated. "Taken where? Like… on a date or something?"

"No, Red! Not a date," Kev scolded through the phone. "The bar's been trashed, the place is a mess, and she's been hauled off. Ezio's in pursuit."

Glasgow, Present Day
Alley off Hope Street – Afternoon

Ezio kept his eyes on the BMW, jaw tight. Beside him, Chiara craned her neck, speaking into the mic, calm and steady.

"Actually, boys, we're no longer in pursuit," she said. "They've stopped. Just off Hope Street. We're casing the joint."

Ezio shot her a sharp look. "You are not casing the joint, Mum. You're staying in the car until we get you home."

"Hi, Ma. How you keeping?" Reddy's voice crackled through, cheerful as ever.

Chiara smiled. "Good, good. How are you boys?"

Chris piped up, clipped. "Fine."

Reddy, oblivious, kept on. "Got a heap of cakes. You into spoken word poetry?"

Chiara snorted. "No, it's crap, Red. But I do like cakes. Full Crumb Bakes?"

"Yeah, but no Cherry Oreo Chip," Reddy sighed.

Ezio threw an incredulous glance at his mother. She waved him off. "That's a shame, son. I'm more of a dark chocolate and Jammie Dodger kind of girl."

Up ahead, two men climbed out of the BMW, moving to the boot.

Ezio tracked them. "If it's alright with the rest of you, can we focus on rescuing our kidnapped friend?"

Chiara shrugged, amused.

"I'm just off Hope Street," Ezio said. "They took the long way round and doubled back."

"Weird," Kev muttered.

"Two of them are out now," Ezio continued. "Heading for the boot."

"Cap, we can be there in ten minutes," Reddy said.

"*No bueno*, big man. You're too far out, and I can't let her out of sight."

A sudden tap on the passenger window made Chiara jump. Ezio turned. Painted fingernails drummed against the glass.

Gina leaned against the car, looking pleased with herself.

Ezio sighed, lowering the window. She stumbled slightly, caught off guard.

"You two alright?" she asked.

Chiara regarded Gina. She still saw her as that same wild teenage girl who used to hang around Ezio—too loud, too bold and far too much trouble. She'd been his first love at nineteen, before his father's sudden death turned the world inside out for Chiara, back when Stefanie was still around and before Ezio left for the Marines. Chiara had known Gina's mother, had known Morris well too—they'd all run in the same circles once. For a while, it had almost felt like family. But Gina had never quite fit the mould Chiara imagined for her son. She didn't trust the girl, and time hadn't softened the feeling much.

Chiara curled her lip. Ezio forced patience. "Yep. All good. Thanks."

"Gina?" Chris's voice crackled through the speaker.

Gina grinned. "Hi, Chris! How's things?"

Ezio exhaled, patience thinning. "Can I help you?"

Gina snorted, "Unlikely." She pointed up the street, "Isn't that your little mate being dragged out of a boot?"

Ezio's eyes snapped back to the alley. Annabelle, a hessian sack yanked over her head, flailed between two men dragging her toward a fire escape. She kicked, writhed—made them work for it.

Ezio's voice dropped. "Guys, they're pulling her out. Positive visual."

"Don't rush in alone," Reddy warned. "We need time to think this through."

Gina twirled her hair, giving Ezio an expectant look. He groaned, glancing at Chiara. She raised an eyebrow.

"Fine," Ezio muttered into the mic. "Sorry, Red. We're moving now."

Ahead, one thug banged on the fire escape door. The other shoved Annabelle inside. The first stepped back, arms crossed, holding his ground.

Chris's voice came through, sharp. "I trust you, mate. Do what you need to. What do you need from us?"

Ezio exchanged looks with Chiara and Gina, then nodded. "Thanks, mate. Head back to Mullholland, help Kev, and get what intel you can." He turned to Gina. "She's covering me."

A sharp inhale sounded before Kev muttered, "Fuck."

Gina's grin widened, savouring it.

Ezio ended the call. "Stay here," he told Chiara.

She nodded. Gina snapped open her knife.

Ezio got out, moving fast. Gina fell in beside him. He glanced at the knife.

"You won't need that," he said. Before she could argue, he plucked it from her hand and bent to one knee, sliding it into his sock.

Gina's gaze darted to the pistol at his waistband. "Oh, but you get toys?"

Ezio ignored her, crossing the street. "We won't need them."

She muttered, smirking. "That's what she said."

Up ahead, the thug barely looked at them. Too late. Gina moved first, quick as a switchblade, her heel cracking against his head. He staggered. Ezio, shocked, managed to improvise and caught him before he could recover, locking the man in a sleeper hold.

The man struggled, then slumped.

Gina bent over him, running her nails mockingly down his cheek before dipping into his pocket. "Nighty night," she purred, twirling the keys she'd just lifted.

Ezio lowered the thug onto the concrete. "Thanks."

Gina quickly unlocked the door. "Yeah."

Ezio dragged the guard inside.

Glasgow, Present Day
Obsidian Lobby – Afternoon

Ezio eased the guard's body into the corner, scanning the dim lobby. Neon light stuttered overhead, bleeding lurid reds and purples into the shadows. A glowing sign pulsed in the gloom: *Obsidian – Your Pleasure is Our Fetish.* Gina raised an eyebrow, smirked.

"You bring me to the nicest places."

"I didn't bring you," Ezio said.

"Whatever. You're welcome." She nudged him toward the stairs. "Go do your job. I'll babysit Sleeping Beauty."

"Fine." He paused to give her a hard look. "No murdering while I'm gone."

She pouted, slipping the knife back into her pocket. "You really have lost your sense of fun."

Ezio shook his head with a faint chuckle as he turned toward the stairwell. "Still, nice to be back in the saddle, eh?"

Gina's expression soured as her gaze swept over him with exaggerated disdain. "Actually, not my kind of ride these days."

Ezio arched an eyebrow. "Noted."

Upstairs, Big Moira selected a bullwhip from the rack. A thicker one this time, the one with diamond studs. Her client—Mr Ewan, her pet piggy for the afternoon—shifted on the punishment bench. His features were lost beneath the hood, but the tension in his limbs said plenty.

"You're flat tonight, Ewan-pig, honestly. This is what you're bringin' to my dungeon? I seen fiercer spirit in that lad who wanted to be tasered in a paddock, he shat himself sideways up a hill and rolled back down greetin' like a slinky leaking shite," she said. "Bless him, the boy shat blood but he *tried*. You? You're an embarrassment. If I don't get two squeals and an oink to the rhythm of gratitude, you'll be wearing the big racoon tail plug."

She turned to the shelf and paused. The tail was missing.

"You want whipped?" she asked. Ewan-pig oinked, eager to please. She dragged the whip across his back, then pinched a fold of skin hard between her nails.

"Where's the fucking tail?" she snapped, and brought the whip down in a crack that drew blood.

Ezio climbed the stairs. Dark wooden doors lined the corridor, most shut tight. Behind one, a whip cracked and something squealed—followed by a low, pitiful oink.

He kept moving.

One door stood wide. Light spilled into the hallway. Ezio stepped in, took in the sight.

The room beyond was all leather and steel. Heavy straps, polished chrome. The scent of sweaty bodies clinging to the walls.

Annabelle hung upside down on a bondage wheel.

She groaned in what seemed like frustration behind the tape. Ezio crossed the room and spun the wheel until they were face to face.

She rolled her eyes.

Ezio ripped the tape from her mouth.

Annabelle winced. "For fuck's sake," she muttered. "Anyone but you. Get out of here."

Ezio examined the bindings. "Gratitude, just give me a second—knots aren't my thing, Madame Pottymouth."

She scowled. "You were in the Navy. Get me out of this."

"It's a trap, isn't it?" He kept his hands moving, undoing the knots.

She nodded. "They want you."

The door creaked open behind them.

Ezio stilled. Annabelle's breath caught.

A figure stepped in, extending a nunchuck to full length.

Ezio and Annabelle exchanged a glance.

"Fuck," they said together.

Jock grinned, rolling the weapon between his fingers. "Well, well… the Capo. I thought you were smart."

Ezio smirked, stepping back. "Oh look, it's a Ninja Turtle head."

"Shut up," Jock snapped.

He swung first. Ezio dodged, feinted left, but the space was tight. Jock caught him clean, a solid blow sending Ezio sprawling.

He scrambled upright, hand landing on a box marked *Used.* He didn't think, just grabbed.

A raccoon-tailed butt plug.

He swung.

It slapped against Jock's face, smearing him with something foul. Jock froze. Ezio froze.

Then the smell hit.

Jock stumbled back, retching. Ezio and Annabelle stared.

Then burst into laughter.

Ezio snatched a metal truncheon from the wall and swung, knocking Jock cold. Still grinning, he moved to Annabelle, working her free.

"Let's go."

Annabelle was still laughing. "You hit him with—he's got shit on his—"

Ezio winced, touching his ribs. "Kev mentioned Albanians?"

A cold voice interrupted from the darkness.

"Not quite. Semenovs."

Ezio turned.

The flat of a shovel walloped the back of his head—the kind of blow that could kill a lesser man. Ezio crumpled as blood seeped through his hair.

Annabelle screamed, thrashing against the hands that held her.

"I'll kill you!" she shrieked. "I'll kill you all!"

Dmitry Semenov stepped into the room, watching her struggle with mild amusement. Behind him, the door swung open.

Gina stumbled into the light, hands bound.

Annabelle's fury turned sharp. "You."

"I'm sorry," said Gina.

"Not sorry enough," Dmitry said. He eyed Gina from head to toe. "Tell Morris I'll be expecting my shipment. No interruptions."

Jock stirred, groaning, his face still smeared with filth.

Dmitry wrinkled his nose, glancing at Ezio's body. "Take that one to visit his father."

Jock hesitated, jaw tightening. "You said you wouldn't kill him."

Dmitry didn't look at him. "You still want paid? Get on with it. Bogdan will show you where."

Then Jock swallowed, nodded. Bogdan stepped in, helping him drag Ezio's body away.

Ezio's phone slipped from his pocket, landing with a dull clatter.

Dmitry stepped forward, ground it under his boot.

"Throw these whores into the street," he said. "Let them spread the word."

Glasgow, Present Day
Alley off Hope Street – Afternoon

In the alley, Jock and Bogdan emerged from the fire escape, hauling Ezio's dead weight between them, his boots dragging. The BMW waited. They hefted him into the open boot of the BMW and slammed it shut.

Chiara blinked, the movement snapping her out of whatever fog she'd slipped into. Her gaze sharpened, fixing on the figures by the car. She blinked again. Her hands, her lap, the dashboard—all briefly unfamiliar.

Jock and Bogdan slid into the BMW and pulled away from the curb. Seconds later, a black SUV rumbled into place, low and heavy. Dmitry stepped into the alley, four thugs in tow. Annabelle and Gina followed, shoved into the street. Hands tied, faces set. Bruised but defiant.

Dmitry took Gina's chin, tilting it up. His grip was careful. Almost curious.

"When my father hears about this…" Gina sneered.

Dmitry cut in smoothly. "I'm counting on it, Miss Kingston." His voice was easy. Amused. "With his prized wolf down, it's time for me to press my advantage."

The slap came hard and clean. Gina rocked sideways, her heel catching on the uneven cobblestones. A sharp snap. She hit the ground hard. Annabelle followed, shoved down beside her.

Another car rolled up as Dmitry boarded the first SUV. His men took the second. Doors slammed shut. The convoy eased down the narrow street, leaving the two women sprawled on the wet ground.

Gina groaned, pushing herself up. Annabelle offered a hand. Gina batted it away. "I'm fine."

"Course you are," Annabelle muttered, wincing as she got to her feet.

They staggered toward Ezio's car. Gina wobbled on the broken heel, then gave up, yanking both shoes off. The Aston Martin's window slid down as they reached it.

Chiara beamed, delighted. "Hello, Annie, my dear!"

Annabelle forced a smile. "Hey, Chiara."

Gina glanced at Annabelle, voice urgent. "You need to get to the Wolves. Ezio could still have a chance. I need to see my father."

Annabelle hesitated. "He looked pretty—"

"There's still a chance!" Gina snapped. "At least, I hope there is. They—they said something about taking him to see his father?"

Chiara's face lit up. "My Tommy? He's at Hawkhead Cemetery." She turned back to Annabelle, full of fondness. "Lovely to see you, Annie." Then her gaze landed on Gina. The warmth cooled. "Oh, you again?"

Gina's mouth twitched. "Yeah, me again."

Chiara looked her over, almost sad. "Filled out like your mother."

Gina blinked. "What?"

"Shame. I miss her."

Gina's tough exterior faltered. She glanced away, fingers tightening around the broken heel. "Me too." She exhaled, a quick, steadying breath. Then her head snapped back up, all sharpness again. "Take her with you," she said to Annabelle. "Get moving."

Annabelle nodded and limped around to the driver's side, easing into the seat. The car pulled away, the rumble of the engine fading into the distance.

Gina watched until it disappeared. She reached down, snapped the other heel, then pulled out her phone, dialling quickly.

"Skip. Bath Street. Now."

She pocketed the phone and limped away.

CHAPTER 3

Glasgow, Present Day
Mullholland Bar – Dusk

Chris and Reddy stepped through the heavy doors of Mullholland, each carrying cake boxes. They stopped, staring at the wreckage. Glass was scattered across the floor, chairs overturned, and the bar was in chaos. Reddy dropped his half-eaten cake in shock, quickly stooping to pick it up and brushing it off.

"What the fuck, Kev?" he said. "Why aren't you running comms for Ezio?"

Kev looked up from behind the bar, pale and shaking. "It was under control," he said. "I had access to his phone mic, but it went dead."

Chris crossed the room and put a hand on Kev's shoulder. "It's alright, mate. Just breathe. Tell us what happened," he said, already pulling out his phone.

Kev took a slow breath. Reddy glanced at Chris. "Can you still track him?" he asked.

Chris tapped his screen. "It's still active, but not moving." He paused, then frowned. "Wait. New message from Annabelle. She's safe. Coming here. Ezio's been taken. Hawkhead Cemetery."

Reddy's jaw tightened. "Right," he said. "Let's go fucking get him."

They ran up the steps and climbed into Reddy's SUV. The tyres screeching as they sped away.

Moments later, two large black SUVs arrived in the same spot. Dmitry Semenov stepped out of the lead vehicle, his eyes sweeping over the bar. He straightened his coat and headed down the basement stairs. His men followed close behind.

Glasgow, Present Day
Shipping Container – Dusk

Inside a rusting shipping container behind St John Operative, Andy McMahon and his wife, Dawn, sat tied to wooden chairs. A haggard pair, faces swollen, knuckles white with fear. Blood had pooled on the stained metal floor.

Marty stepped back, shaking the ache from his hand. Andy coughed up two more teeth.

Outside, Morris leaned against the container, arms folded, watching with faint amusement. Eammon stood beside Marty, grinning as he rolled a pair of pliers in his palm.

"Talk," Eammon hissed.

Nothing.

He stepped over to Dawn, crouched beside her, and slid his fingers across her calf. He took his time peeling off the shoe, then hooked a finger into the top of her stocking. She gasped, and he tore it down the seam. "Talk or I start with this," he said, gripping her foot close to his face—close enough it seemed as if he might lick it. "I'll take the little toe. Then, brave man, maybe I make you eat it."

Andy gagged, then spat blood. "Name's McMahon. I run a barge. Pick up spares for the carriers, that's all. I was paid to ferry a few crates. I never opened them. Just did the job. Didn't know what I was in the middle of till we pulled back from Faslane toward Greenock. Then… I get a video call. Bloke in my living room with a gun on my wife and kids."

Eammon pushed the pliers into Andy's chin. "Keep going."

Morris rolled his eyes. "Christ's sake, Eammon…" He looked to Dawn. "He's not the bright one, is he?"

She sobbed, voice shaking. "Andy will talk, Mr Kingston, please, he'll tell you."

Marty's hands twitched, his breath shallow as he stood rigid. Morris stepped forward into the container, resting a hand on Marty's shoulder. Eammon cast them a wary glance.

"Too close to home?" he asked, quiet.

Marty's jaw tightened. "I'm good." He gestured toward Andy. "Just thinking, the lack of teeth might not help him talk."

Morris snorted, acknowledging the practicality. "He'll talk eventually." He gave Marty's shoulder a light squeeze. "Go on. Grab us some drinks."

Eammon puffed up his chest. "I've got this, mate," he crooned.

Andy lifted his head. "The Chapel of St Mahew. Out near Cardross. It's old, hidden in trees. My old man used to be the priest there. Still lives in the presbytery so it was easy to have a few lads help me stash the crates. Dad is the quiet sort, no questions asked."

He coughed again, barely breathing. "So the lads helped me get the crates inside and I watched them leave, made sure they were gone. The tabernacle, it's hollow. There's a safe inside. I was told where to look for a package, what to take and where to put it. I never opened it. I didn't look. I swear."

The container fell silent.

Eammon's smirk faded. He dropped the pliers. They hit the floor with a dull clang.

Morris grinned. "See? Not so hard, was it?"

Glasgow, Present Day
Hope Street – Dusk

Unbalanced without her heels, Gina hobbled along Hope Street. A sleek, blacked-out SUV rolled up behind her, its engine purring softly. The passenger window lowered, revealing Skip, her ever-stoic bodyguard.

"Where to, boss?" he asked, leaning slightly out of the window.

Gina yanked the door open and hauled herself into the seat beside him. Her usually composed appearance was frayed, her tone clipped. "Take me to my father's stupid Masonic Hall. He and that idiot Marty have been dodging my calls all day."

Skip's brow lifted. "You alright?"

"Just drive, Skip."

Her glare stayed fixed straight ahead, leaving no room for further questions.

Skip nodded, his face tightening with quiet concern as he shifted the SUV into gear. The vehicle pulled away smoothly, tyres gliding over the damp asphalt. Skip said nothing, but kept glancing at her— nervous as if she might explode. The tension thickening between them.

Glasgow, Present Day
Just Outside Hawkhead Cemetery – Dusk

Just beyond the boundary wall, where the cemetery gave way to rough ground, Ezio's limp form was hauled from the boot of the BMW. A few feet back, rows of gravestones stretched long and staggered, old stones leaning beside newer slabs, like crooked teeth half-swallowed by moss. Beyond the tree line ahead, shipyard cranes pierced the sky. The damp air clung to everything, turned soil and the faint tang of rust. Earthworms writhed underfoot, disturbed by the digging. The grave sat crooked on a rise at the highest point of the hill, dug into no-man's-land behind the farthest family plots. No visitors out here. No birds. Just wind.

"Nothing personal, mate," Jock muttered, his voice tight with remorse.

Bogdan shot him a glance, incredulous. "He's dead. Why apologise?"

Jock hesitated. "Maybe for my own conscience." He looked away, his grip tightening on Ezio's lifeless body. "Didn't think Semenov would actually go through with it."

With a grunt, they dumped Ezio into the shallow grave. His body landed with a sickening thud.

"Just needed the cash," Jock muttered, running a hand through his hair. He stood there, wavering. "Not sure it's worth much now."

Bogdan rolled his eyes, yanking two shovels from the trunk. "Still, nice night for it. Feels Christmassy."

Jock took a shovel, his expression uneasy, and they began heaving dirt over the motionless figure below.

Glasgow, Present Day
Mullholland Bar – Evening

Dmitry Semenov lounged in Ezio's red leather chair, a smugness rolling off him as thick as his Brut Musk aftershave. His eyes drifted over the office's gentlemanly decor, sneering at the refinement. Across from him, Kev sat rigid, his repulsion barely masked.

The door creaked open behind them. Kev didn't turn. Heavy footsteps, the sound of struggle. Annabelle was dragged in, dumped into the chair beside him. Chiara was handled more carefully, set in a chair against the wall. The thugs left, the door slamming behind them.

Dmitry rocked back in the chair, turning lazily. "Ezio…that a Catholic name?"

Chiara, distant, tilted her head. "Do you go to church, son?"

Kev didn't blink. "Word to the wise, Semenov, best not to bring that up around him. It's something of a trigger."

Dmitry's smile widened. "That won't be an issue. He's been…dealt with."

Chiara's gaze settled on Dmitry, steady. "You really should, you know."

Dmitry smirked. Kev caught it, understood that tell for what it was. He let a slow grin spread. "She's right. Should've thought this through." Kev felt more confident now his voice was quiet, measured. "Ezio's been 'dealt with' before." A pause. Then, a shrug. "Never seems to stick."

Chiara chuckled softly. Dmitry shifted, unsure if she was all there or playing him.

Kev turned to Annabelle. She sat pale, knees together, fingers laced on her lap. Her eyes fixed on the floor. Something dark, hollow in her face.

"Annabelle?" Kev asked, dreading the answer. "Surely not?"

Annabelle's hands shook. "I saw…" A whisper, then silence. Tears welled, choking her words.

Kev's jaw clenched. "No…no, Annie. This can't be right."

Chiara stared at the floor, clicking her heels together. Nobody spoke.

Glasgow, Present Day
Just Outside Hawkhead Cemetery – Evening

Dirt shifted. Earth stirred. Ezio's hands clawed through the soil, shoving against the weight above. Each push stronger, meeting less resistance than the last.

A few yards away, Bogdan and Jock stood at the rear of the BMW, in no real rush to leave. The forest pressed in around them, the border wall of Hawkhead Cemetery just behind. They packed their spades into the trunk, oblivious.

Bogdan patted his pocket, producing a small package and grinning. "Got a light?"

Jock reached into his jacket and flipped open a neat-looking Zippo. "If you've got one to spare."

Bogdan chuckled, sparked the lighter, and lit two cigarettes, handing one over.

Jock lifted his cigarette, turning it between his fingers before raising it. "To the Capo."

Bogdan leaned in, grin widening. "To new friends. Nostrovia!"

Jock forced a little joy into his features, taking a long drag. But his eyes lingered on Bogdan's. Wary.

Bogdan nodded at Jock's waistband. "Really is a nice piece."

Jock glanced down, let out a chuckle. "Forgot I'd taken it." He pulled the gun, striking a poor imitation of a movie spy.

Bogdan laughed, amused.

In the shadows, Ezio rose from the earth, his face caked in dirt. The blade of Gina's knife caught the moonlight, flashing for an instant before he lunged. The knife buried deep in Jock's shoulder. A scream ripped from him. Jock's grip failed, the gun slipping from his grip as pain surged through his shoulder.

Ezio caught it mid fall, clamping Jock's fingers around the handle. He wrenched them over the trigger, forcing the barrel toward Bogdan. "You shoot him."

A shot rang out. Bogdan staggered back, clutching his gut, eyes wide with disbelief.

Ezio twisted Jock's wrist, peeled the gun from his grasp and forced Jock's arm upward. The butt of the pistol crashed into Jock's face with a crunch. He went down, out cold before he hit the ground.

Ezio staggered, caught himself, moved toward the cemetery wall. He reached the low stone boundary, dragged himself over, stopping only to brace himself against a tall gravestone. He looked out—Glasgow's lights spread below, shimmering under the night sky. As if it were a city with nothing to hide.

Through the haze, recognition.

I know this place.

He steadied himself, turned to the inscription on the grandest stone, the one with the best view.

Here lies beloved husband, father, uncle, and dearest friend – Tommy Trevino.
A man who would never knowingly pass you in the street.
RIP – 10-09-1958 to 11-06-1999 – Forever missed.

Ezio pressed his forehead against the stone. His voice barely a whisper. "Hey, Dad."

Bruised and aching, he straightened. Took a step. Then another. Each one with a little more strength.

Glasgow, Present Day
St John Operative – Evening

Behind the bar of St John Operative, Masonic lodge and Morris Kingston's regular place of business, Marty balanced a tray of recently refilled whisky glasses. Morris sat among ledgers, a laptop open in front of him. Eammon leaned over a large, yellowed map spread across the table, attempting to trace the lines.

The door swung open. Gina stormed in, Skip trailing nervously behind.

Marty froze, took her in, dishevelled, wild-eyed. He smirked. "What the hell happened to you?"

Gina didn't answer. She strode straight to him, snatched a glass from his tray.

Morris stood, grinning. "Darling."

She downed the whisky in one go and spun to face her father. "Don't give me that. Where have you been?"

Morris stepped forward, arms open, but she shoved him back, her anger flaring. He chuckled, brushing it off.

"Not today, love," he murmured. "Your old dad's got some emotional business on his plate."

Gina scoffed. "You have emotions?"

Morris laughed, unbothered. He strolled past Marty, poured himself another drink, and then slid glasses to the others as they gathered round. Eammon, Marty and Skip took theirs. Gina folded her arms.

Morris raised his glass. "Come on, all of you. Making good men better."

The others echoed the toast, raising their glasses. Four men drank. Gina rolled her eyes.

Morris set his glass down with a sharp clack. "You two have your instructions," he said, nodding at Marty and Eammon.

They nodded back and turned to leave.

Gina waved a dismissive hand toward the door. "Off you trot, errand boy."

Marty smirked. "Whatever, cunt. At least I'm not out knifing kids."

Gina stiffened. "They weren't kids."

Marty's grin widened. "Sure. Don't split your knickers." He nodded at her torn trousers. "Oh wait, looks like you already have."

Eammon sniggered.

Morris stepped between them, shaking his head. "All right, lovebirds," he said, patronising. Then, to Marty, "You've got a package to retrieve."

Eammon tossed a mock salute. "Yes, boss."

Morris scoffed. "Fuck off, Eammon."

Marty snickered, jerking his head toward the door. "Come on, you twat."

They left. Gina watched them go, jaw tight. Then turned back to Morris, eyes burning. "What package?"

Morris poured himself another drink, unfazed. "The Semenov cache. Ezio's gun shipment."

Her arms folded tighter. "Guns? Really? You don't think I know what you're up to?"

Morris raised his glass, winking. "One team, darling. They're just picking up Ezio and heading to Cardross. Easy job."

Gina shook her head. "Picking up Ezio? That won't be easy."

Morris froze mid-sip. His frown was small, but it was there. "What do you mean?"

Glasgow, Present Day
Hawkhead Cemetery – Evening

Ezio staggered down the cemetery path, swaying like a drunk, clothes caked with dirt, blood dried in his hair. The SUV's headlights caught his shambling silhouette as it rolled to a stop.

Chris and Reddy leapt out onto the pavement.

Ezio buckled. Reddy grabbed him, keeping him upright.

"How the fuck are you still on your feet?" Reddy said.

"What?" Ezio rasped. "Driver's seat, bud."

Chris stepped in, blocking him. "No chance. Head trauma, no oxygen in the boot, and it looks like someone fucking buried you. Ezio, Jesus—you should be dead."

Ezio steadied himself on the bonnet. "I got lucky, mate. Simple as that." Pointed vaguely behind him, "Air pocket under a… a tree root. No time for patching up."

Reddy chortled. "Still wearing that Kevlar skull they gave you at Sennybridge, eh? All bone, no brains—good thing you're pretty."

He waved them off and pointed up the hill. "Get moving. Handle it. There's a car up there you can use."

Reddy raised a brow. "The gunshot?"

"You heard it?"

Chris glanced up the hill. "Yeah. Won't be long before the police catch wind."

Ezio slumped into the driver's seat, wincing as he pulled his Colt from his waistband. He tossed it onto the passenger seat. "Car at the top. BMW. Two marks. Deal with it. I'm heading to Mulholland."

Chris half smiled. "Alright. But we want a full debrief in an hour, yeah?"

Ezio nodded, grunted.

Chris nudged Reddy. "Come on, you big lump."

Reddy chuckled, a low, rolling laugh. The kind you'd hear in a bar right before the glasses started flying. He clapped Ezio on the shoulder, then jogged up the hill with Chris.

Ezio started the engine. Took a breath. Then roasted off into the night.

Glasgow, Present Day
Mullholland Bar – Evening

Kev braced himself against Ezio's desk, shaking his head. He turned, searching Annabelle's face. Disbelief sat heavy in his voice.

"Annabelle… Did you actually see it?"

Tears streaked her cheeks. She nodded, hollow-eyed.

Gunfire erupted from the bar outside. Screams followed.

The room tensed. Annabelle's wide eyes snapped to Kev.

He barely reacted. Just smiled. Calm. Composed. His faith restored. "Time for the show." He winked.

Chiara cheered gleefully from behind.

The lock on the door burst apart with a violent blast. The door flew open.

Ezio entered, Colt raised, elbows bent, the gun held steady. Dead calm. Eyes tracking the barrel as he scanned the room. Ezio lowered the gun, and smiled that trademark grin.

"Hi, Mum." Ezio glanced at Chiara. "Shouldn't you be home by now?"

Chiara shrugged. "Can't be helped."

Dmitry's hands went up, palms out. His face a picture of pleading.

Ezio strolled forward, clapping Kev's shoulder as he passed. He tossed the Colt onto the desk, rounding it casually. Kev and Annabelle flinched.

Dmitry glanced from the gun back to Ezio. His shoulders eased.

Ezio barely acknowledged him. His fingers drifted over the desk, papers, a pen, a snow globe. Buckingham Palace. He picked it up, held it to the amber light.

Dmitry forced a nervous smile. Nodded, like it was a prize worth admiring.

Ezio smiled back. Then smashed the globe into Dmitry's head.

Dmitry collapsed, sliding down the chair, eyes rolling back. Ezio followed, fists pounding down. The two men vanished behind the desk. The beating had a rhythm, sickening. Wet. Bone meeting solid glass.

Blood sprayed up in bursts, spattering the desk, the walls. The globe reappeared occasionally in Ezio's hand, now slick with gore, rising and falling with brutal efficiency.

Then silence.

Ezio emerged, breath steady. More blood on him now. Maybe more than before, if that was possible.

A tooth clung to his shoulder. He swatted at it, but it held on.

Annabelle and Kev stared, mouths slack.

Ezio adjusted his seat, sighing.

Chiara broke the silence. "I'll be needing a lift home, then." She dusted herself off and strolled out to the main bar.

On Bath Street outside Mullholland, the traffic was non-existent. A dead winter night, midweek.

Marty's SUV rolled to a stop behind three others. He and Eammon stepped out, eyeing the row of expensive parked cars.

Halfway down the basement steps, Marty stopped. Peered through the window.

"Something's off," he muttered.

Eammon crouched, took a look. His face changed. "Holy fuck."

"Yeah." Marty's eyes narrowed. "Wait in the car. In case we need to move fast."

Eammon hesitated. Then nodded, retreating. Marty adjusted the grip on his gun and moved inside.

The bar was wrecked.

Chiara stood at the counter, watching him.

Marty's shoulders sagged. He let go of his weapon.

"Marty!" Chiara beamed as she strode across to him. Chiara pinched his cheek hard before pulling him into an unsolicited hug. "You lovely boy."

Kev and Annabelle emerged from the office, flustered.

Kev's eyes narrowed. "McHendry. What do you want?"

Marty freed himself from Chiara's grip, smoothing his ruffled hair. "The Semenov cache." He took in the wreckage. "I need Ezio. Now."

Annabelle folded her arms. "Marty, do you even know what just happened?"

Marty glanced at the shattered glass, the overturned furniture. "Renovations?"

Kev wasn't amused. "He's in the office. You should go talk to him."

Marty nodded, moving toward the door.

Inside, the office smelled of blood. Dmitry Semenov's ridiculous shiny purple loafers stuck out from behind the desk.

Ezio buttoned a fresh shirt. Barely looked up. "The shipment?"

Marty blinked. Glanced at the mess. "Yeah. How'd you—?"

"Minor issue." Ezio brushed past him. Didn't slow.

Marty hesitated. Stared at the desk. He didn't want to look over. But couldn't help himself.

Ezio was already out the door. "The lads will sort it. Let's go."

Back in the bar, Chiara sipped cool wine, watching Kev stash the bottle in the fridge.

Annabelle surveyed the wreckage. "Lot of mess."

Chiara traced the condensation on her glass. "Nothing a wee bit of elbow grease won't fix, dear."

The front door burst open.

Chris and Reddy strode in, hauling Jock between them. They threw him to the floor in front of the bar.

Kev and Annabelle's eyes widened.

Chiara took another sip. Unfazed.

"And look," she murmured. "The boys brought a helper."

Ezio entered.

Marty stopped near the office door, phone in hand. He dialled, letting it ring as he surveyed the scene.

Ezio's gaze landed on Jock. The man was crumpled on the floor, his shoulder wrapped in a bloodied shirt— it looked like Bogdan's.

Jock met Ezio's stare, pleading.

"You want to do it, boss?" Reddy asked.

Ezio's expression darkened.

Jock swallowed hard. "Please," he begged, voice shaking. "It was just a job. I didn't think…"

Chiara cut him off, unimpressed. "You didn't think what?"

She aimed a swift kick at his side.

Jock let out a choked yelp.

"It's the package," he managed, grimacing. "Has everyone on edge. I didn't know they'd try to kill you. Let me work for you."

Chris scoffed. "Forget it."

Jock's desperation spiked. "I'm as good as dead if you let me go. I'll prove myself."

Reddy grinned. "Who said anything about letting you go?"

Ezio rubbed his temple. Said nothing. Just stared at Jock.

Weighing the situation.

Alone on the threshold of Ezio's office, Marty held the phone to his ear. His voice was low.

"Place is a bombsite and he's fairly beaten up, but he's adamant about coming with us."

Morris crackled back, cool, calculating. "I'll bet he is."

Marty's gaze scanned over the wreckage. "Can't blame him. I don't think he suspects we know what's in that shipment, or that it's been hidden elsewhere."

He nudged a broken glass with the toe of his boot.

"It's strange."

He let the words sit for a beat, then nodded to himself. "I'll let you know when we have it."

Marty ended the call, throwing one last look at those purple loafers before slipping the phone into his pocket.

Ezio stood between Chris and Reddy. Appraising Jock, he scanned the group. "I'll take Kev. You two handle the clean-up."

Marty appeared as Reddy cast a dubious glance at Jock, still slumped on the floor against the bar.

"Yeah, and what about him?"

Ezio exhaled, exasperated. "We don't waste life. We're better than that."

Chiara and Chris nodded. Reddy's expression soured, but he didn't argue.

Ezio turned to Jock. "You need to make yourself useful. Start with your boss's brains in my office."

Jock nodded fast, eager to prove himself.

Marty folded his arms. "Morris won't like it."

Ezio's response was instant. "Fuck him." His tone left no room for debate, drawing smirks and stifled chuckles from around the room.

Chiara raised her wine glass, a slow smile forming. "I'll stay to supervise. I've cleaned up worse."

She took a long swig. The others exchanged glances.

Ezio sighed, conceding. "She's right. There was no one better, once upon a time."

Reddy clapped Ezio's shoulder and led Jock off to his new duties.

Annabelle strode in from the back, fresh clothes, hair fixed, a spark in her eye. "Can we go now?"

Ezio arched a brow. "It's me and Kev. Not *we*."

Annabelle pouted. "I'm traumatized. I'm coming." She winked at Marty, who looked as puzzled as Ezio.

Marty shrugged. "Sure, the engine's running."

Ezio kept his gaze on her, unimpressed. "Fine," he sighed. "Off you go. I'll be there in a second. I need a word with your crush."

Annabelle rolled her eyes. "He's not…" She trailed off as Kev pulled her away, but managed to shoot Ezio a defiant look before disappearing upstairs.

Ezio turned to Marty. "Can I trust you?"

Marty blinked. "Me?"

"Yeah, you." Ezio straightened, eyes locked on Marty. "I'm putting people on the line here."

Marty scoffed. "You've got a nerve." His face darkened. "And you don't know the half of it."

Ezio frowned. "What do you mean?"

Marty looked away, frustration showing. "You don't want to know."

"Actually, I do," said Ezio.

Marty shook his head. "You think you've got it tough? My wife was murdered. I've got a daughter who thinks she's looking after me. When do you ever deal with real pain and loss?" He didn't wait for an answer. "Yet you swan back here, back to this city, and it all comes so easily."

Ezio inhaled slowly, glancing at Chiara behind the bar. She poured another glass of wine and watched them.

Marty followed his eyes. Chiara raised her glass, smiling.

Ezio turned back. "I know it's not the same. Not even close. But I'm responsible for them now. We're broke, and we need this. If you're not screwing me over, you and Parker are always welcome here."

Marty hesitated, caught off guard. "We are on the same side," he muttered. "More than you realize."

Ezio grinned, punched Marty's shoulder. "That's all I needed to know."

They headed for the door, Chiara watching with satisfaction as they jogged up the basement steps.

Outside on Bath Street, Marty nodded toward the Semenov vehicles parked along the curb. "Better get rid of those."

Ezio shrugged. "Reddy's got a gypsy contact. He'll flip them."

Marty winced. "I feel for the gypsies."

As they reached Marty's SUV, Ezio spotted Annabelle and Kev already in the back. Eammon sat up front, looking smug.

Ezio frowned. "What's that doing here?"

Marty smirked. "That? That's an Eammon."

Ezio sighed. "Yeah, I can see that. But why's it in the front?"

Marty grinned. "Say hi, Eammon."

Eammon leaned back, tossing a cocky salute. "Hi, Eammon."

Ezio stared at him. "Right then?"

Eammon looked confused. "Right then, what?"

Marty jerked a thumb at the back seat. "In the back with you."

Grumbling, Eammon climbed out.

Annabelle huffed. "I need the window," she said, shoving him back.

Eammon scowled. "But you're the smallest."

"Be a gentleman, Eammon," said Marty.

Eammon sulked his way to the middle seat. Marty and Ezio exchanged a quiet chuckle.

Annabelle settled by the window, flashing Marty a grateful smile in the rear-view mirror. "Thanks, Marty."

Marty grinned as Eammon and Kev jostled for space.

With everyone finally on board, Marty pulled away. He and Ezio shared an amused look as the SUV disappeared into the night.

CHAPTER 4

Glasgow, Present Day
St John Operative – Evening

Morris sat behind his laptop, surrounded by open ledgers. He placed his phone on the table as Marty ended the call, barely glancing up as the door behind the bar swung open.

Gina entered, changed out of her earlier mess. Low-cut top, trainers, cargo trousers. Practical.

She didn't waste time. "That stupid little shadow of yours?"

Morris nodded, still scanning the figures. "Marty? Aye. And he's one hell of an earner."

He finally looked up, offering a smug smile. "Those Wolves might be clever, but nothing gets past your old dad." He winked.

Gina's eyes narrowed. "You wouldn't send Ezio on something small. What's going on?"

Morris smiled, smoothly shifting gears. "Come here. If you're taking over, you need to be across this."

Gina sighed but slid into the seat beside him. "Don't you pay people to handle your accounts?"

Morris leaned in, tapping a finger against a ledger. "This is the accounts of the accounts. Numbers never lie."

Gina rolled up her sleeves, scanning the figures. "Guess this is part of the job," she muttered. "Grooming me for the big chair?"

Morris let out a deep laugh. "That started years ago."

She grinned, pride glinting in her eyes as she squirmed, settling beside him.

Glasgow, Present Day
M8 Motorway – Night

The air inside the SUV was thick with boredom. Marty steered off the M8, heading toward the Erskine Bridge.

Kev stirred, blinking groggily. Annabelle sighed, shifting in her seat.

"Marty…" She glanced over, hopeful. "I need a break. Can we stop somewhere?"

Eammon groaned. "We're on a schedule."

Annabelle shot him a look. "Nobody asked you." She tucked her hair behind her ear, turning back to Marty, all sugar. "Please, Marty?"

Marty met her eyes in the rear-view mirror. "Sorry, Annie. We're under twenty minutes out. Can you hold on a wee bit?"

She fluttered her lashes, a mock surrender. A smile broke through. "Okay, Marty. I can do that."

Eammon fidgeted, his phone slipping in and out of his hand.

Glasgow, Present Day
St John Operative – Night

Gina sat hunched over Morris's computer, eyes scanning files. Across the room, Morris busied himself with the coffee, watching her.

"What'll you take in it?"

She barely heard him. "Something isn't right here."

Morris raised an eyebrow. "What's that?"

Her eyes didn't leave the screen. She answered rubbing her temple. "Milk, two sugars."

He smirked, brought the coffees over, set one beside her.

"So, Ezio. The prodigal son returned—eventually." He leaned back, watching for any reaction. "Thoughts?"

Gina's gaze drifted from the screen to Morris. "He's not the same person," she said quietly. "I'm sorry. I know you want him to be, but…he's different."

Morris leaned back, still smiling.

She studied him, eyes narrowing. "Yet, you always have a plan."

"I do." His eyes held that knowing glint.

She didn't hesitate. "Did you plan this?"

"Not exactly." He ran a finger along the rim of his cup. "Sometimes, you just create the right conditions."

Something shifted in Gina's expression. A thought piecing itself together.

Morris watched, amused. "Sometimes, you just have to create the right conditions."

The words hung in the air. Gina's mind turned, memory fragments snapping into place. As she thought, the chaos of the past began to make sense.

Morris sipped his coffee, eyes still on her. "What happened to him out there, nobody deserves that. I tried to protect him. But…he's a tool now, shaped to be wielded. And soon, he'll be yours."

Morris took a slow sip of his coffee, then set the cup down deliberately. "Can you work with that? Make him think he's your partner when I'm gone?"

Gina shook her head, stunned. A laugh escaped her. "I don't believe…"

"Now, now," Morris waved a hand, amused. "Don't be upset."

She glanced at him, almost in admiration. "Upset? No." A slow grin of her own. "It's…brilliant."

Morris lifted his coffee in a toast.

Glasgow, Present Day
Old Church Cardross – Night

Marty's SUV rolled onto a dirt path behind the church, headlights dimmed. Ezio caught sight of a small, rough track leading into the woods.

Annabelle saw it too. She felt his gaze, met it. Her big hazel eyes held his green eyes. A small tilt of her head. Agreement.

One by one, they stepped out. Marty and Eammon pulled reinforced duffel bags from the boot.

Eammon scowled. "Why're we parking here?"

Marty stayed calm. "Basics. Keep the car hidden."

Eammon exhaled, unimpressed. "Suppose."

They moved toward the rear entrance of the church. Annabelle and Kev bickered, voices low, words lost in the shuffle.

Ezio hung back, scanning the trees, the path, the shadows. Then Eammon.

Something about him was off. Felt wrong.

Glasgow, Present Day
St John Operative – Night

Empty coffee cups littered the table. Gina pored over paperwork, flipping between documents, scrolling through spreadsheets. Across the room, Morris stood by the dartboard, throwing darts. Each one hit its mark.

"Didn't mean for you to dig so deep," he said, glancing over. "Come throw a few with your old man."

Gina scowled at the screen. "Dad, something isn't right here."

Morris paused mid-throw. "Are you onto something?"

She looked up. "I don't want to alarm you, but… this American account, it doesn't look right."

Morris closed the distance, looming over her. "You don't question that account. Ever."

Gina's jaw tightened. "I'm not stupid. I know it's the syndicate. All those rumours, I stopped questioning those years ago."

His stare didn't waver. "Then don't start now."

She held his gaze, voice steady. "It's not going out. It's coming in."

Morris leaned closer. "That can't be. Coming in where?"

Gina scrolled, her fingers moving fast. "It's spread across several places. But tie them together?" She turned to him. "We've got a rat."

Glasgow, Present Day
Old Church Cardross – Night

Ezio stepped through the rear entrance, checked his phone. "These old buildings, they sure don't build them like they used to. I've lost signal."

Inside, the church was gutted. Where pews once stood, crates filled the space, four of them, stacked in neat rows at the centre of the main hall. The same four-digit designations as he'd had Reddy mark them with, military-style, spray-painted in stencil.

Torchlight from his phone swept over them. He searched for one crate in particular.

Eammon tossed a duffel bag at Kev's feet. Marty lobbed one to Ezio, tone light.

"The three bears?" Ezio muttered, catching it.

Marty chuckled. "Hibernating. Hopefully."

Behind the altar, Marty worked a hidden safe tucked inside the old tabernacle. Ezio, paying him no attention, pried open a crate—5210. The very one he was looking for. His hands ran over the rough plywood interior, searching for the familiar weight of a velvet pouch.

Kev leaned in, voice low. "Where's the package? I thought it was in here."

Eammon paced by the window, fidgeting with his phone, stealing glances out through the stained glass.

"It has to be here." Ezio kept searching, breath tight.

Kev frowned. "Is it the correct box?" He ran a hand over the stencil. "ASCII value 5,210, yeah?"

Ezio shone the torch over the designation. "It's the right one. Reddy stencilled the box while I put it here myself." His eyes met Kev's.

"Somebody moved it," Ezio murmured.

They turned just as Marty slid something into his pocket, the tabernacle closing with a quiet click.

Glasgow, Present Day
Mullholland Bar – Night

Chris and Reddy were hunched over their cards. Across the room, Jock hauled heavy refuse sacks from the office, sweat gleaming on his forehead.

Chiara peeled off her rubber gloves, tossing them into a bucket of red-stained water. She stretched, wandered behind the bar, and scanned the brass bar taps.

"What'll you boys have?" Hands on her hips. "Been a while since I poured a pint."

Reddy brightened. "Now you're talking!"

Chris barely looked up. "Red, we need to stay alert, mate."

Chiara gave him an easy smile. "Say no more." She turned to the coffee machine, running a hand over it as if greeting an old friend. "I used to make a mean cappuccino."

Jock reappeared, wiping his brow. "Everything is sorted in there."

"Good lad. Coffee break?"

Jock hesitated, then nodded. "That'd be lovely."

"Go on then, sit with those scoundrels. I'll sort you out." She winked, and he dropped into a seat.

Reddy shot him a glare but turned back to his cards.

Chris slapped down his hand. "Ha! Gotcha!"

Reddy barely glanced up. "No, you haven't."

Chris grinned, flipped his hand with a flourish. "Learn to count, mate."

Reddy grumbled and tossed a biscotti across the table. Chris scooped it up like a poker chip.

"Cheatin' wee wank," Reddy muttered.

"Wanker or liar, mate, your choice," Chris said, dealing again.

Reddy grabbed another biscotti, then turned toward Chiara, hopeful, like a puppy waiting for a treat. "Got any more of these, Mah?"

Before she could answer, Chris snatched it from his hand, grinning as he took a bite.

"Between these, those cookies, and God knows what else, you need to get your fat arse back in the gym."

Jock raised an eyebrow. "What's all this about alert and on point?"

Reddy shoved another biscuit into his mouth, scowling. "We don't trust that wee Irish goon."

Jock moved quickly, swiping the next biscuit before Reddy's hand could reach it.

Chris turned serious. "It's our shipment. This level of interference feels wrong."

"Suspicious?" Jock frowned.

Reddy and Chris exchanged looks.

"Not necessarily," Chris wrinkled his nose. "But it stinks."

"Last time Ezio went off on his own…" Reddy let the words hang.

Jock's face dropped.

"Ah, shit," Reddy muttered. A hint of regret.

Jock stared at the table. "I deserve that."

Chris shook his head. "No, you don't. You did your job."

Reddy nudged him, smirking. "Worked out, at least. I've got someone to beat at cards now."

The tension cracked. Jock rolled his eyes. "In your dreams, fatty."

Chris burst into laughter. Reddy swung a playful jab into Jock's shoulder.

Jock winced. His stab wound still fresh.

"Oops," Reddy said. Not quite an apology.

Chiara returned, balancing mugs of coffee and a plate of cookies from Full Crumb Bakes.

"Got to keep your energy up, silly big lump," she teased, nudging his arm.

Reddy flushed. "Thanks, Mah."

Glasgow, Present Day
St John Operative – Night

Gina scanned the paperwork, face pale. She swallowed hard, eyes glancing at her father.

"That run with Marty and Ezio…" Her voice caught. "It's not just guns, is it?"

Morris didn't react. He only stared at the page on the ledger. But she caught the twitch in his jaw.

She jabbed a finger at the laptop screen. "Tell me you didn't send Eammon with them."

Morris closed his eyes. His shoulders dropped just a fraction. He felt it land.

"Fuck, Dad." Gina gripped the edge of the desk. "Fucking fuck." She exhaled sharply. "What's at that church?"

Glasgow, Present Day
Old Church Cardross – Night

Four of six bags were already loaded into the boot of Marty's SUV. The last two sat zipped in the hall.

Ezio and Kev exchanged glances, eyes darting to Annabelle. She shook her head, shrugged.

All three of them wide eyed.

Ezio groaned, shifting the weight of the bags. The church door slammed, the impact rattling through the stone walls.

They froze.

"Eammon?" Ezio called.

Then, headlights flared outside, flooding the hall with white-hot light.

Marty's shoulders slumped, frustration tightening his face as garbled shouts rang out.

"Fuck," he muttered.

Kev snapped to attention. "The package."

"Secure it, Kev," Ezio ordered, dropping his bags. Marty dropped his too.

Ezio knelt, unzipping his bag.

"Okay, you're with me. Annie, stay back, stow the gear. If this goes south, grab as many bags as you can. Got it?"

Annabelle nodded, face set. She reached into a bag, tossed Kev a pistol with two spare mags.

Ezio pulled out an MP5, tossed another to Marty. Checked his grip on his weapon and snapped out the telescopic stock.

"Marty, you cover the door. I'll hit the tree line. We overlap, no mistakes."

Marty blew out a breath and shifted his grip on the gun. "Got it."

They rushed to the main entrance, Kev stacking up behind Ezio.

Marty steadied himself. Then kicked the door open and fired into the dark.

Gunfire cracked back. Bullets splintered the wood around them. Marty quickly retreated inside.

Glasgow, Present Day
St John Operative – Night

Morris met Gina's glare, his own stare bleak. Her face was pale, tight with frustration.

"Diamonds?" she said. "You burned Ezio over fucking diamonds? Fuck me! We've been played, Dad."

Morris rubbed his thumb across his knuckles, slow. "He burned himself. Thought he could fool me. Half the city's after that fortune." His teeth clenched. "Eammon, that weasel—"

"It's bigger than that," Gina cut in. "If Marty doesn't have them, and Eammon does…?"

Morris lowered his gaze to the table. His fury simmered.

"He's taken them to the Syndicate," he said. "They've turned on me."

Gina exhaled, steady. "Alright. These Syndicate types—they're not gangsters. They're business people. We either get the diamonds, or we protect Ezio who can maybe protect us. Maybe both. That's our only chance."

Morris nodded, though the anger hadn't left him. "Contact his team. I'll brief Skip."

"Wait, just—wait." Gina stepped toward him. "You stood up to the Syndicate before. You kept heroin off the Clyde."

"They respected that," Morris said. "They understand power."

She shook her head. "Dad, it's Ezio. It always was. The diamonds—yes, he stole them but they were moved without him. He never knew where. They weren't his. They were never his. The Syndicate planted him in that op. That Moroccan compound—it wasn't just a terrorist pit. It was logistics. Diamonds out. Chemicals in. CIA funnelled the intelligence, sure, but they were chasing the stones just as much. Must have told them that the mission was to free the captives. Stands to reason. But the diamonds? That was the real mission."

Morris turned, walked to the back of the room. Drove his fist into the wall. Plaster cracked and dropped.

"Fucking Eammon," he muttered.

Gina didn't flinch. "Ezio thought he was in control. Why not take something for himself, set up a bar, and lead a better life. He smuggled the diamonds back in weapons crates on a Royal Navy carrier or whatever.

Bribed a supply barge to lift them off. Figured it was clean."

She paced once, slow.

"But what if the Syndicate saw it coming? What if they paid the barge captain more, rerouted the shipment to Cardross, stashed it in that church? That would explain why Ezio never knew where they landed. Why he needed us to tell him."

She stopped, facing Morris again.

Morris's mind raced. "That couple Marty interrogated. That man had a boat out of Greenock."

"That's it, they let him do all the heavy lifting. He thought he was acting on initiative. But if I'm right, those diamonds were never his to steal."

Morris said nothing. Stared at the wall, as if it might answer back.

Gina's voice dropped.

"He was never in control, Dad. Just a loose end. And he doesn't even know it."

Glasgow, Present Day
Old Church Cardross – Night

Dark figures spilled from the parked vehicles along the tree line, moving fast, guns up. They took cover behind the remnants of old crumbling stone walls.

At the front, Alexei Semenov swaggered forward.

"Come on out!" His voice was mocking. "Hand over Trevino and the package, maybe we can make a little deal."

Marty didn't hesitate. "Fuck off!"

Ezio glanced at Kev, gave a nod. Kev chambered a round.

Marty whispered a count, "One… two…"

Ezio planted his feet, tensed. "Moving."

"Move!" Marty snapped. Gunfire cracked through the night.

Ezio and Kev bolted into the church grounds, sprinting for a giant oak tree. They hit it hard, dropped low. Ezio fired.

"Back in! Contact, two o'clock!"

"Moving!" Marty's voice stayed steady.

Ezio was about to shift position when something struck his neck. A dull thump.

His hand shot to the spot instinctively, grasped a small, strange object and pulled it free—a tranquiliser dart. The plastic reservoir behind the needle was empty, glistening with the last of its contents. One of the red stabilisers was bent from the impact. A faint chemical smell lingered—alcohol, maybe.

He stared at it, dazed.

A canister round bounced against the giant oak.

"Frag!"

He and Kev scrambled just as the explosion ripped through, throwing up dirt and debris. Ezio's vision blurred, his head swimming.

Voices broke through the haze.

"He's here! Grab an arm!" Annabelle.

Marty grunted, hauling Ezio's weight through the underbrush. Annabelle noticed the dart, snatched it from his fingers, stuffed it into her pocket, and tightened her grip on his arm.

"Come on, Trevino," Marty hissed. "Don't you let me down, boy, not to these bastards."

Glasgow, Present Day
Mullholland Bar – Night

Chris, Reddy, and Jock sat around the table, empty coffee cups scattered between them.

Reddy chomped happily on a Double Caramel Log stuffed cookie. Chris stacked biscotti into a pile, eyes narrowing at his winnings.

Jock gathered the mugs, arranging them onto a tray.

The landline rang.

All three turned to Chiara behind the bar.

Reddy squinted. "We have a landline?"

Chiara shrugged.

Chris sighed. "It's a business, mate. People still call to book."

Chiara picked up. Her expression changed instantly.

"It's Gina!" she called.

Chris rolled his eyes. "Tell her we're fully booked."

Reddy and Jock chuckled.

Chiara didn't.

Her grip tightened on the phone. "Ezio's been ambushed."

Reddy slammed his hands on the table. "Knew it. Fucking knew it!"

Chris was already moving. "Have her send the location to my phone."

Chiara relayed the message, hung up, then rubbed her templcs.

"Eammon's involved," she said grimly. "Working with the Syndicate. Against Morris."

Jock's face paled. "Oh, this is bad."

Reddy scoffed. "We've dealt with worse than him, pal."

Jock paled, shaking his head.

"No—not like this. The Syndicate, they're the hidden power behind everything."

Chris spun on Reddy.

"We have to move."

Glasgow, Present Day
Old Church Cardross – Night

Marty's SUV tore across the church grounds, kicking up dirt as it hit the rough track behind the building. The vehicle's suspension jarred.

Marty gripped the wheel, knuckles white. In the back, Annabelle fought to keep Ezio pinned down, his body heavy, groggy.

"Fucking cane it!" she yelled, bracing as the car jolted over another bump.

Ezio mumbled, barely conscious. "No… Kev… Plan HELO… he said HELO."

Marty grimaced into the mirror. A sharp drop loomed ahead.

"Hold tight, this is going to be fucking horrible."

The SUV hurtled down the narrow farm track, swallowed by the trees as the darkness closed in.

Chapter 5

Glasgow, Present Day
Mullholland Bar – Night

Chris checked his gear. Reddy packed the essentials.

Chris's phone buzzed. He snatched it up, already tense.

Reddy shot him a look. "Answer it."

Chris already had. He listened, nodded. "Got it. How bad? Okay. Send your location."

He placed the phone on the table, ran a hand over his face.

"They got Ezio out."

Reddy slumped. "Thank Christ. And Kev?"

Chris winced. "He's alive but unconscious. He and Ezio took a grenade blast, they had to leave Kev behind, pinned down under a fucking tree."

Reddy's breath caught. "Fuck, that's no fucking good."

Chris nodded. "Ezio took the brunt of it. Annabelle and Marty dragged him out, but Kev… he was just trapped."

Jock swore under his breath.

Chris's eyes narrowed, a glint of something behind them.

"But Kev did make one last request before they left him." He looked at Reddy, a slow grin spreading.

"He said, 'HELO'."

Reddy bared his teeth, knuckles whitening. "Let's give them hell."

Chris picked up the phone, tucked it between his shoulder and ear, moving toward the bar.

"We're coming."

Glasgow, Present Day
Old Church Cardross – Night

The ground outside the old church was a wreck of torn-up dirt and splintered trees.

Alexei Semenov moved between the cars parked before the remnants of old crumbling stone walls. One of his men stepped into his path, hand to his chest.

"Alexei, uh, Mr Semenov, sir," the thug faltered. "It's not safe yet."

Alexei slapped him. The crack echoed and the thug stumbled back.

"I'll decide when it's safe." He grabbed the thug by the collar, yanked him close. "They've got my diamonds, and Trevino needs to pay, fast, for the demise of my dearly departed brother."

He cackled, shoved the man aside, and kept walking.

Eammon, up ahead, slowed. He stopped short, his foot brushing something heavy.

Kev.

Bloodied, motionless.

Eammon called out. "Alexei! We got one!"

Two men wrenched Kev's arms, struggling to haul him free. Another pair ran up, straining to lift the tree trunk pinning him down.

They dragged Kev's limp body toward the church.

Alexei clapped Eammon on the shoulder as he passed. "Well done."

Eammon's look soured, but he said nothing.

Then he followed inside.

Glasgow, Present Day
Mullholland Bar – Night

Chris stood at the bar, typing rapidly on his laptop, phone wedged between his shoulder and ear.

Reddy and Jock packed ropes and gear into bags. Chiara watched from nearby.

"One second," Chris muttered, fingers flying over the keys. "I've got something that'll make this a lot easier."

Reddy zipped a bag shut, shot him a look. "You set to go yet?"

"Almost." Chris put the phone on speaker. "Annie, I've opened Kev's phone mic and sent a URL. Anyone can log in and listen. Just remember, it's live, so be careful who gets the link, okay. How is he?"

Annabelle's voice crackled over the speaker. "He's groggy, no bad wounds, just a puncture mark on his neck. Found a dart too. Keeps asking for his kit so he can get Kev, but Chris… he's in no condition."

Chiara stepped forward, epinephrine pen in hand, offering it without a word.

Reddy rolled his eyes, snatched it from her. "I'll take care of that." He leaned toward the phone. "Did you get the package?"

"Just a boot full of weapons," Annabelle said. "The package must still be in the church."

Chris and Reddy shared a look.

Reddy slung the last bag over his shoulder. "That'll work for now."

Chris hit send. "Link's going to Marty's phone. You can patch it through the car speakers."

Glasgow, Present Day
A82 Trunk Road – Night

Marty skidded the SUV off the dirt track onto the main road, the big engine growling beneath him.

In the back, Ezio sprawled, bloodied and dazed, his hand pawing uselessly at Annabelle's arm.

"What is it?" She leaned closer.

Ezio mumbled, voice thick. "RV at QEU…"

Annabelle frowned. "What are you on about?"

Marty kept his eyes on the road, but something clicked.

"He wants you to pass it on," he said over his shoulder.

Annabelle groaned. "Fine."

Glasgow, Present Day
Mullholland Bar – Night

Annabelle's voice came back apologetic. "Sorry, Chris, he keeps saying 'RV at QEU'. I don't know what the fuck that means."

Reddy frowned. "He wants the hospital?"

Chris checked the GPS. "Makes sense. It's right between us. Based on your route, we can meet you at Queen Elizabeth."

No hesitation. They grabbed the gear and bolted for the door, pounding up the steps to the street above.

Chiara, unbothered, poured herself another glass of viognier. She raised it slightly, a silent salute as they left.

Glasgow, Present Day
Old Church Cardross – Night

Kev sat slumped in the wooden chair, arms tied, head pounding.

Eammon stood over him. Alexei Semenov lingered behind, a circle of thugs watching from the shadows of the darkened hall.

Eammon crouched, tipped Kev's chin up with feigned concern.

Alexei growled. "Hit him."

Eammon held up a hand. "Relax. He's coming around."

Kev jerked his head back, glaring. Eammon leaned in, voice smooth, coaxing.

"We know where you live, where you work… just tell us where they're headed. Where did Marty plan to stash the package?"

Kev's mocking laugh cut through the room. The thugs glanced at each other, shifting, unsettled.

Kev tilted his head. "You really think Marty's working with us?"

Eammon studied him, intrigued.

"It was possible," he said lightly. "Morris has lost the Syndicate's backing. They've appointed a new trustee to run the city."

Glasgow, Present Day
St John Operative – Night

Morris and Gina faced each other at the bar, Skip standing by Gina's side.

Skip holstered his weapon, watching as Morris read a text. Gina, meanwhile, tucked a blade into her jacket.

Morris pointed at her, eyes fixed on his screen. "No. You wait in reserve. This part isn't our fight."

Gina nodded at his phone. "Whatever, who is it?"

"Marty." Morris scanned the message. "They got Ezio out, but he wants to go back in."

"For the diamonds, I'd wager." Gina smiled darkly. "And most probably to kill that rat Eammon."

Morris's face tightened. He read the message again.

"Eammon's got Kev."

Gina shrugged. "So what?"

Morris tapped his phone, a small smile forming. "Smart lad, Marty. They've opened Kev's phone mic. They can hear everything. I'll send the link. Skip, set it up on the car speakers."

Skip nodded. "We can do that."

"Good. Let's go," Gina snapped, ready to move.

"Stop."

Morris's voice cut through the room. His stare pinned Gina in place.

"You don't go in unless the Wolves have cleared the place. Kev means nothing to us. Skip, if she tries anything before it's safe, stop her. Or don't come back."

Skip nodded. "Yes, boss."

Gina hummed, thinking. "Kev might be nothing, but intel on the Syndicate… that is valuable."

Morris gave a single nod. "If you get the chance, extract Eammon. But Semenov doesn't leave alive, no matter what."

Gina and Skip shared a look, both nodding.

"Got it," Gina said.

As they reached the door, Morris made a call.

"It's me. Get the Syndicate. We need a conference."

He listened, unimpressed.

"Don't give me that. You and the Syndicate owe me. Half an hour. If you want your family to see next week, you'll be there."

He hung up, staring at the empty bar.

Slowly, he reached for his coat. Slid it on. He felt it's weight settle on his shoulders.

Calmly, just like his daughter, Morris slipped a blade into a concealed pocket.

Hidden, but close.

Glasgow, Present Day
Old Church Cardross – Night

Alexei Semenov loomed over Kev, blade catching the light, a sneer curling his mouth.

"We have all the time in the world."

Kev met his gaze, unflinching, then threw Eammon a smirk.

"That so?"

Alexei's brow lifted. "Why protect them? Especially Trevino? He's a thief, he steals and kills. The man has no honour."

"You're right," said Kev. "He has killed, you should remember that. He's not perfect, I've seen that too."

Kev shifted, the haze of his mind drifting to the past.

"The morning after the first day I met him changed everything. I caught them—him, Chris, Reddy, all three. Walked into their tent, I just strode right on in, unannounced. Massive canvas thing, luxury compared to the rest of the camp. Officers turned a blind eye. The Wolves lived better than the rest. Because of who they were. What they could do. I walked in on them… and my whole life changed."

Morocco, One Year Earlier
Ben Guerir Air Base – Night

Kev stood outside the Wolves' tent, nerves chewing at him.
He stared at the phone in his hand—a photo: Ezio Trevino all smouldering intensity as usual, snapping a selfie, battle-worn and filthy. Kev in the background, just as rough but grinning like an idiot.

"He's your friend now," Kev muttered. "Just a man."

He pushed through the tent flap and stopped dead.

Ezio hunched at the bunk's edge, a locket clutched around one fist, a velvet pouch dangling from a string in the other hand.

Reddy's hand rested on his shoulder. Chris hovered nearby, grim.

The Wolf of the base, their legend, and he was sobbing like a broken boy.

Kev coughed. "Sorry to intrude. Bad time?"

Reddy spun, fists clenched. "Out. Now. Fuck off, wee man."

He grabbed Kev by the throat, but Ezio's voice rasped across the room. "Red, no. Bring him in. He deserves to see."

Reddy grunted, grabbed Kev's collar instead, and dumped him onto the bunk across from Ezio.

Chris shifted. "You sure about this, Cap?"

Ezio wiped his face, tucked the locket into a pocket, and held out the velvet pouch.

Kev inhaled sharply. "Is that—?"

"It is," Ezio said. "All that chaos out there. All that loss. And here's me, the hero. Sitting with this. Not what you thought I was, eh?"

Kev leaned forward. "With respect, sir… fuck that. Fuck it all to hell."

"Easy there, Kev." Chris sat beside Ezio. "He's right, Cap. You're just not yourself. I know it hurts but we saved lives. We do plenty of good."

Ezio let out a bitter laugh. "Good? That's what we tell ourselves. We kill. We win. We get called heroes. But what do we actually change?"

He held the pouch higher.

"If this is anything to go by, we're pawns. We don't do good. We work for fucking tyrants."

Reddy bristled. "Stop it, Cap!"

Chris raised a hand to quiet him. "Maybe we've always known it, deep down. Yeah, we're addicted to the rush, what's wrong with that? But what's the alternative?"

"We stop," Ezio said. "We break the cycle. I'm done. They've taken everything."

Kev shifted on the bunk. "Might I?"

All eyes turned to him. For the first time, they listened. Even Ezio, pleading without words.

Kev cleared his throat. "I don't have the answers. I know this place is fucked. But maybe… there's somewhere else. A place where doing good actually counts. Where people care."

Silence fell. Heads dropped.

"There's one place," Chris said. "All three of us call it home."

Reddy groaned. "You can't mean—"

"Yep."

Reddy sat down hard. "Oh, fuck off. Not fucking Scotland. Not fucking Glasgow."

Chris grinned. "Think about it. My family's there. Ezio, you've got your mother and sister—"

Ezio cut in. "Stefanie has moved on, mate. She's too big for Glasgow, and there are too many ghosts. I ran from that city before it could either turn me into a monster, or kill me like it killed my father."

Chris shook his head. "Just listen, hear me out. You were younger then. Alone.

Now you've got us. And you're the Wolf, mate. Glasgow won't kill you and there's nothing in this world that would make you a monster. We might even save it."

He leaned closer. "We can't shift what's in that pouch alone. It's useless without Inaya's contacts in the States. But Morris? We could use him to somehow launder the lot. Save what's left of our souls. Clean up the city and maybe even…"

Ezio stared at the pouch. His knuckles whitened. "Do some good," he whispered.

"Boom," said Chris, throwing up his hands.

Reddy muttered something obscene and let his head drop with a groan. "Fine. But it will take a lot of fucking drink. I'll need truckloads of rum, you hear me?"

They looked at Kev. He shrugged. "Mind if I tag along?"

Chris raised a brow. "You'd move to Glasgow? You ever been there, mate? Aren't you from California?"

Kev smiled faintly. "It's not like the movies, Chris. It's changed over the years, but when I transitioned… decided to live as a man… a lot of people I loved didn't stick around. My wife and I…"

He turned to Ezio. "My little tribe and me, Ezio, we need a fresh start."

Reddy slapped his back. "You can have some of my rum to help you adjust."

The four of them laughed.

Kev grinned. "Come on, Glasgow can't be worse than Barstow."

Reddy snorted. "On the contrary, dear Kev. Glasgow's full of the best human beings you'll ever meet. Salt of the earth. Aggressively friendly. Glasgow's miles better."

Glasgow, Present Day
Old Church Cardross – Night

Kev leaned back in his chair. "That's why I'm here. He's the reason I moved to Scotland. Ezio Trevino took me in. Chris and Reddy made me family. Annabelle came later, he saved her too. We are a family and nothing can separate us."

Eammon considered this a moment. "Not exactly a ringing endorsement of character though, is it?"

He turned to Semenov.

"You've literally just told us the man's a despicable fucking thief and a murderer," Alexei said.

"You don't know him at all, do you?" Kev's voice was steady. "I'd die for that man. We all would and you want to know why? Fine. I'll tell you."

His gaze drifted. Memories stirred.

Morocco, One Year Earlier
Ben Guerir Air Base – Dusk

The desert sky burned low, fading from deep oranges into a dusty haze.

Inaya punched Ezio's chest, playful, her sapphire eyes catching the last of the light. She grinned, caught his hand.

"Come on, Mr Wolf. Walk me to my plane."

Ezio's face softened. Emerald irises catching hints of gold. Inaya had always loved that—how something hard could still shine. She often found herself lost in the mystery of those eyes.

He looked her over, charm giving way to concern.

"Always happy to be of service, madam CIA."

They walked the tarmac in step, her grip tighter than usual. Ahead, the C-130 Hercules waited, engines winding up.

"They moved it up," he said. "I didn't know."

"I didn't either," she replied, half smiling. "Intel dropped fast. One of those 'no one else can do it' situations."

His gaze lingered on her. "You're sure you're fit for this?"

"I wouldn't be on this bird if I wasn't. Besides, someone's got to make your job look easy." She squeezed his hand. "Last-minute intel on the package. But I'm the only cover asset we have. I'm in too deep. I know the compound, I know the players. No time to swap me out."

He didn't answer, not right away.

She leaned closer, brushed his cheek with her fingers. "I have more top secret intel for you, Captain."

She glanced at the ramp, then placed a hand on her stomach. Her fingers lingered.

"This will be the last time."

Ezio looked at her stomach, a brief moment of disbelief. Then it hit. He knew.

"You can't mean…"

Inaya nodded once.

"Yes, I am," she whispered. "Only just found out. I'm fine. And so is this." Her hand remained at her belly. "I checked. There's no trauma. No risk. It's early. I'm cleared for the jump."

A beat passed. Then, her smile radiant, she said, "And the package, it's in that compound."

Ezio stepped back, staring at her. Heart caught somewhere between awe and dread.

She smiled again, more softly this time. "I can do this. Then we're done. We get out. We build something normal. Or try."

Ezio laughed in disbelief, swept her up, spinning her as she shrieked.

"We can leave, Ezio! After this, we leave. You cook breakfast. I sleep in." She kissed his jaw. "And you learn to make proper tea."

He laughed harder, pulled her close and squeezed her tight.

"Maybe I'll throw in a cold Tennents."

She wrinkled her nose as she pulled back in his grip. "For breakfast? I spit in your Tennents. Only Macallan."

His grin faded, just slightly.

"Are you sure?" he asked again.

Her reply was quiet. "This is who I am. Just like it's who you are. We don't get to pick peaceful lives. We just make them, one piece at a time."

"You'll be right behind me?" she asked.

Ezio swallowed hard. "Always," he said. "Same plan as before, you drop in, we light those fuckers up, pull you out and hit them even harder from the air.

She held his shoulders, grounding him. "The secondary objective, it's them. The ones we've been searching for. Women. Children. Brainwashed, like I was. Families held in shipping containers, forced labour. We pull them out, Ezio. That matters."

He squeezed her hand. She kissed him, then turned. The ramp lifted, engines roaring. Her lips shaped the words: *I love you.*

Ezio cupped his hands, shouting above the noise. "Olive-oil. Elephant-shoe. I love you more!"

She laughed. She loved him—and that single fact meant everything to Ezio Trevino.

Ezio didn't move. He stood there for what seemed like an eternity as the plane roared forward and lifted into the desert sky.

Reddy appeared beside him, breathless. Chris jogged up behind, panting, hands on knees.

Ezio clapped a hand to Reddy's shoulder. Pulled Chris upright.

"It'll be okay," he said. "This will work."

They nodded, caught in the gravity of a man who made them believe it.

Glasgow, Present Day
Old Church Cardross – Night

Kev's voice filled the hushed church hall. Quiet. Certain.

"She was pregnant."

The room held still. Alexei's expression barely changed, but Kev saw it— that moment of doubt.

"She was about to jump from that plane to save lives," Kev went on. "If this had been about the package, Ezio would've stopped her. But he knew. Knew what it meant to her."

His gaze swept the room, settling on Alexei.

"Inaya was rescued the same way. She lost her mother. Ezio understood that, losing a parent and the need to make it right."

Eammon shifted. Alexei's jaw tensed.

Neither sure whether to be moved or unnerved.

Glasgow, Present Day
A82 Trunk Road – Night

Marty took the exit for the Erskine Bridge.

In the back, Ezio groaned as the vehicle lurched. Annabelle leaned over him, pressing him back as he reached for her hand.

"Be fucking still," she whispered.

Ezio smirked, barely conscious. He crooked a finger, drawing her closer. His voice was a rasp.

"I need you to do something."

She frowned, leaning closer. He whispered.

Her expression shifted. Shock.

"That can't work," she murmured. "It's... Ezio, that is insane."

Ezio's grip tightened around her hand, a faint smile ghosting his lips before his body slackened.

Marty glanced over his shoulder. "What did he say?"

Annabelle stared out the window, gripping her phone.

"Screw it," she muttered. "I'm making another call."

Glasgow, Present Day
Kingston Bridge M8 – Night

Skip gripped the wheel, knuckles white. Kev's mic feed came through crystal clear, broken only by the hum of the engine and the soft sound of gears shifting. City lights flared and faded across their faces.

Gina stared ahead, her phone lighting up in her lap.

"You ready?"

Skip nodded, eyes fixed on the road. "Ready."

"Good boy." She didn't need to look to know how that landed.

Gina read Marty's text aloud.

"They have a plan. Meet us at QEU."

She exhaled, loud, unimpressed.

"Change of plan, Skip. We're meeting them here."

She punched in the new location.

Glasgow, Present Day
M8 Motorway – Night

Reddy shifted his gear around in the back, checking straps, inspecting rope, sorting equipment.

Chris, up front in the passenger's seat, met Jock's eye. A silent nod toward the car stereo, Kev's voice still coming through clear, sharp.

"What he said, about rescuing people…" Chris gestured, eyes steady. "That's us. We save people, Jock. You're one of us now."

Silence. Then Reddy's voice cut through, grinning.

"That's right, poo breath."

Jock's eyebrows lifted. "You heard about that?"

Reddy's laugh boomed through the SUV. Chris snickered.

Jock held out a moment, then gave in. Leaned back. Grinned.

Glasgow, Present Day
Old Church Cardross – Night

Kev, still bound, stared them all down. His voice filled the room. Steady. Calm.

"Saving people… that's all Ezio ever wanted. Chris told me once. Ezio, he'd never admit it himself."

Alexei scoffed, he rubbed his temple as if swatting away a headache.

"Killing my brother. That is a strange way to save people." He exhaled, weary. "Anyway, even if that were true, what's it got to do with us?"

Kev met his eye. Unfazed.

"Everything. It means he's coming. And you. You're already dead." Kev said this without bravado. It was just a fact. "Whatever's keeping you here, Alexei, whatever it is? It is not worth your lives."

Alexei laughed, loud and grating. His shoulders shaking.

Eammon didn't join in. He just watched Kev, head tilted, a hint of pity in his expression.

"For fuck's sake, O'Connell," Eammon sneered. "Look around you. You're tied to a chair with no shoes on. What's the point here?"

Glasgow, Present Day
M898 Motorway – Night

Lights flashed across Marty's face, sharp angles in the dark. He gripped the wheel, locked in concentration as the city sprawled bright and endless to his left.

Kev's voice came clearly through the speakers. Steady. Certain. "Yeah, there is."

Annabelle glanced at Ezio, unconscious across her lap, then lifted her phone like an actor preparing to step onstage.

Marty muttered under his breath. "This is insane."

She held up a finger, shushing him, then gasped into the phone.

"My name? Uh, it's… Cookie!"

She winced. Too late now.

Marty raised an eyebrow.

Annabelle cleared her throat, pushing through the lie.

"Yes, Cookie Molar," she said, voice tight with forced distress. "It's my husband. He's hurt, erm, his legs."

On the other end, the operator's keyboard clattered. "Okay, Cookie, where are you?"

Annabelle put the call on speaker so Marty could hear. She filled her voice with panic.

"Near Cardross? An old church. We were hill-walking."

The typing didn't stop.

"That's quite remote," the operator said. "Can you describe his condition?"

"He's wheezing, can't get up. I tried to help, but he screamed." She paused, scrambling for thought. "I think… I think I punctured his lung."

Ezio stirred, a low groan escaping him.

The operator straightened. Annabelle could hear it in her voice.

"Stay calm, Cookie. The air ambulance will be ready in fifteen minutes. You need to keep him warm, keep him conscious."

Annabelle glanced at the rear-view mirror, a smug little grin forming.

Marty shook his head. Disbelieving. Amused.

"Bravo, Madame," he muttered.

CHAPTER 6

Glasgow, Present Day
Queen Elizabeth University Hospital Car Park – Night

Jock killed the engine, the hospital car park empty around them.

"What now?" He shifted, uneasy.

Reddy leaned back, hands behind his head. "Now we wait."

Chris settled in, nodding at the stereo.

"And listen."

Silence. Then Kev's voice came through the speakers, transmitted from his phone.

Glasgow, Present Day
Old Church Cardross – Night

Kev sat, motionless, the dim light cutting hard lines across his face. Alexei and Eammon stared, frustration simmering between them.

Kev flexed his fingers against the rope, testing.

"That evening, I met Ezio Trevino for the first time."

Alexei scowled. "You hadn't even met him? Why are we listening to this shit?"

Kev looked between them, unfazed.

"Because he was dealing with all of it. Right then. Right there."

Kev let the silence stretch, watching them.

"And still…"

Morocco, One Year Earlier
Ben Guerir Air Base – Night

Kev scanned the transport authorization, flipping through the pages. Primary objective: Five of Diamonds. His stomach knotted.

His breath hitched. "Oh no." He flipped the page, eyes locking on to the next line. Secondary objective: extraction of innocents.

Kev's grip tightened on the clipboard. The second objective rarely mattered.

As he pondered, his fingers brushed the family photo taped to the dashboard. He shook the doubt away, scanned the last line. His eyes widened.

"Wait, no way." He read the names aloud, pulse spiking. "Captain Ezio Trevino. Sergeant Alessandro Rossini. Warrant Officer Chris Hunter."

His mouth went dry. "The Wolf."

A shadow moved outside. Kev looked up.

Captain Ezio Trevino himself. In the flesh. Nonchalantly leant against the door of Kev's Humvee, calm, unreadable. Behind him, his Wolves loomed, solid as statues.

Kev fumbled, dropping the clipboard to his lap.

"Corporal?" Ezio's voice had that smooth, Scottish edge. "You're our driver tonight?"

Kev straightened. "Yes, sir. Ah, Kev. Corporal O'Connell, I mean."

Ezio grinned, quick, easy. "No worries, Kev." He stuck his hand through the window. "You call me Ezio."

Kev clasped Ezio's hand, warmth and confidence in the grip. "Uh, yes, sir—Wolf—Captain, I mean—Ezio."

Behind them, Reddy and Chris climbed into the back, watching—amused.

Kev reddened, looking down. He jumped as the passenger door clanged shut. Ezio settled in.

Kev let out a shaky breath. "Sorry. I'll stop calling you *sir*."

Ezio gave him a wry look. "Excuse me, Corporal? Why? I earned it, didn't I?"

Kev blinked. From the back, Chris chuckled, punched his arm.

"Don't let him rattle you, mate. Call him Cindy if you want."

Kev exhaled a nervous titter of a laugh. Ezio turned, voice low, flat. "Do not call me Cindy."

Reddy and Chris lost it. Kev's face burned. "Oh no, I'm sorry."

Ezio grinned, shaking his head. "Relax."

Kev slumped forward over the wheel, letting out a relieved chuckle.

With a shake of his head, he put the vehicle in gear and the convoy rolled out, headlights slicing into the dark. Chris leaned over to Reddy. "Seen the Cap do this before."

"Works, though," Reddy muttered. "Gets 'em motivated."

Kev beamed, glancing back. "Can't believe it. The Wolf. In my car."

Reddy shouted, "We're all the Wolf!"

Chris slugged him on the arm.

"Pipe down, genius."

Reddy shrugged. "It was my idea."

Kev, barely listening, grinned. "Wait till I tell my family. Can I get a selfie? After the mission, of course."

"No," Ezio said.

Kev muttered, still buzzing, "Right."

Ezio looked at the dashboard photo, a woman— two kids, all smiles.

"Is this them?"

Kev nodded, pride in his voice. "Yep, that's my squad."

Ezio's eyes lingered, something unreadable in them. "Beautiful family, Kev. You're their hero, you know."

Kev smirked. "Oh, yes, sir. I know."

Ezio's expression shifted. "Sorry."

Kev frowned. "Sir?"

"The selfie. We won't get to take it." Ezio's tone was softer now. "I'll be gone. You're just taking us in."

Kev swallowed. "Right. I see."

Ezio turned to the road. "We've got birds inbound. We secure the target, recover our contact and light the place up, exfil by air. You handle the captives."

Kev frowned. "If they come. They said to wait until after you left, so I thought…" He trailed off, shrugged. "Never mind, just the driver. I should know better."

Ezio's eyes snapped to him. "Just the driver?"

Kev stiffened.

"Corporal." Ezio nodded toward the road ahead. "You are the rescue. You're the hero to these women and kids. I'm just here for the show."

Kev sat up straighter, pride stiffening his spine.

Reddy, barely above a whisper, "Buttons."

Chris nodded. "Yep. Another Buttons."

Ezio turned back to Kev. "Can we count on you?"

Kev's grin stretched ear to ear. "Hell, yeah!"

Ezio held out a fist. "Hell, yeah."

From the back, two fists shot forward. "Hell, yeah, Buttons!"

Kev gave Reddy a look, eyebrow raised.

The Humvee sped through the open desert, dust rising behind them. Ezio reclined his seat, ready for a pre-op nap.

Kev gripped the wheel. Heart pounding.

Glasgow, Present Day
Old Church Cardross – Night

Alexei sneered. "Buttons?"

Kev smiled slightly but said nothing. Alexei leaned in.

Behind him, Eammon hunched forward, rubbing his face. Before glancing up at Kev, uneasy.

Glasgow, Present Day
M8 Motorway – Night

Annabelle curled herself over Ezio, arms firm around his shoulders. Kev's every word sinking deep. Her pride in him swelled.

Marty shot her a look in the rear-view, one brow lifting. That name, Buttons, registered.

Annabelle caught it, met his gaze with a quiet smile. "Just listen," she whispered. "It's coming."

Glasgow, Present Day
Old Church Cardross – Night

Alexei frowned, disbelief written all over his face. "Why the hell did he call you Buttons?"

Kev chuckled, his satisfaction rising. "Reddy… he's got a degree in psychology."

Alexei snorted. "Get out of here."

Kev held his gaze, unshaken. "Seriously. The wolf symbols? That was all him—psychological warfare. Designed to make the enemy believe in something bigger. A bogeyman waiting out there," Kev nodded toward the large stained window, "in the dark."

A pause. Alexei's eyes shifted, just slightly. Catching on the reflected images of the room's occupants in the glass.

"It worked," Kev said. "Better than he expected."

No one spoke. Thugs glanced toward the door. A shared, uneasy shift.

"It's still working now," Kev went on, his grin slow, deliberate. "The name Buttons, that was how they reminded themselves to keep an eye on me. I was green, trusted but not yet tested. It meant they were watching, making sure I could handle myself… without getting us all killed, of course."

Alexei's bravado wavered. Eammon shifting beside him. Kev didn't flinch

Alexei's eyes tightened, fox-like wrinkles forming as curiosity warred with unease. "So, they used it for others?"

Kev let his weight sink into the chair, bare feet scuffing playfully against the cold floor. Watching Alexei bite. "Annabelle was Buttons for a while too." His voice carried a trace of pride. "We've got a new one now."

A pause, a knowing smile. "But he won't be Buttons for long."

Glasgow, Present Day
M8 Motorway – Night

Annabelle pulled Ezio closer, grip firm, holding onto something precious.

Marty caught the movement in the mirror. Annabelle's wink.

Something clicked.

Buttons.

He'd thought it was some piss-taking in-joke, another nickname to throw around. But hearing Kev now, the way he said it… pride in his voice, like it meant something. They'd been looking out for him. Ezio, Annabelle, all of them.

His grip tightened on the wheel. He felt a bit daft for not seeing it sooner.

But mostly he felt something settle in his chest. Something he'd been missing for a long time. Something warm. Something good.

Glasgow, Present Day
Pollock Country Park – Night

Morris walked up to the bench. Joe, his syndicate contact, sat hunched, the streetlight throwing yellow over his resentful sneer.

Joe tilted his head, eyes glinting. "I don't know who you think you are, but the syndicate's done with you."

Morris closed the gap, standing over him. "Oh, come now," he said, smooth but cold. "You know exactly what I think of myself."

The sneer twitched.

Joe glanced away. "Yeah," he muttered. "You said it."

Morris settled beside him, close enough to steal the air. He cracked his knuckles, slow, deliberate. "I did, didn't I?" His voice dragged like a slow blade over stone.

Glasgow, Present Day
Queen Elizabeth University Hospital Car Park – Night

Skip's SUV rolled up beside Reddy's. Marty's screeched in right after, stopping sharp.

Skip glanced at Gina. "Here we are."

Gina didn't look at him. She was already studying the set-up, eyes cold, calculating. "I see that, Skip."

Reddy marched straight for Marty's SUV, the others following. Annabelle wrestled with the rear door, struggling against Ezio's dead weight. Reddy snorted, unimpressed. He reached in, grabbed Ezio, and dragged him out, dropping him hard onto the pavement. The thud echoed through the near-empty car park.

Jock and Skip exchanged glances. Marty lingered by the boot of his SUV, watching.

Gina covered her mouth, staring at Ezio. "We're fucked."

Annabelle's voice cut through the tension. "See? He can't go with you."

Chris knelt, rummaging through the med kit, calm. Gina ran a hand through her hair, frustration boiling over. "We are completely screwed."

"Bullshit," Reddy snapped. "We need him." He crouched, slapped Ezio hard across the face. Nothing. Reddy the maniac cackled— then, without warning, drove an epinephrine syringe straight into Ezio's chest.

Gina and Annabelle recoiled. Chris smirked, holding up a hand. "Wait for it."

Ezio gasped. His body jolted upright like he'd been shocked back to life. Reddy grabbed Ezio by the shoulders, howling, "He's alive!" Reddy and Chris burst into fits of laughter, the sound echoing through the night. Annabelle exhaled hard, relief written all over her face.

Ezio coughed, chest heaving. A grin fought its way through his breathlessness. "You dickheads."

Annabelle chuckled, shaking her head. The laughter spread through the group.

Gina didn't catch it. "None of you are normal." She folded her arms, but the smirk gave her away.

Skip and Reddy hoisted Ezio to his feet. He swayed once, steadied.

Chris clapped Ezio on the shoulder. "We heard the call. It's HELO, yeah?" He patted his pack. "Brought the device."

Reddy grinned, pulled out a massage gun. Jock unfolded a tripod.

Annabelle squinted at the set-up. "Wait—what the fuck is HELO?"

"High-speed entry via low-altitude operation," said Reddy, powering up the massage gun. It buzzed to life as he pointed it at her like a pistol.

Annabelle batted it aside. "And that requires a massage gun?"

"It's tactical," Reddy grinned. "Thump, thump, thump—put it on the roof, aim it down, and it sounds like a chopper coming in. Scares the shit out of them."

Ezio frowned. "You won't need that." He stretched his shoulders, rolled his neck. "I've got a better idea. Full-scale assault."

Gina stepped in front of him. "Full-scale?" She arched an eyebrow. "You'll need more than a stupid massage gun and high hopes."

Ezio nodded at Marty. Marty grinned. "I've got you covered." He popped the boot. The duffel bags inside gaped open, weapons glinting under the streetlight.

Gina exhaled sharply. "Fair play, rat boy." She reached in, pulled out a sniper rifle, tested the weight. "This is mine. And I. Am fucking well in."

Skip shot her a worried glance. Reddy let out a low, rolling chuckle, clearly approving.

Ezio's grin widened. "Glad you approve. But you haven't seen anything yet."

He nodded to Chris, who was already unfolding a set of tactical plans onto the car bonnet. The group gathered, leaning in as Ezio took command.

He tapped the map. "First things, flirt." He winked at Gina and Annabelle. "I need a big favour from you girls."

Then Kev's voice came through Marty's SUV speakers, clear and certain. "Ezio's gift isn't just getting people to follow orders. It's making them want do the right thing, and backing them when they do."

A laugh followed, smooth, mocking. Alexei Semenov "Oh really?"

Kev's response, in that light breezy Californian accent, came through all confidence and filled the air. "Really."

Morocco, One Year Earlier
Desert, Near Tangier – Night

Kev's eyes stayed on the road, the desert stretching endlessly ahead. Beside him, Ezio stirred, groggy. He rubbed his face, shook off the last of sleep.

"All right, Kev." His voice was rough. "I'm sending these people back to you. No matter what."

Kev glanced sideways. Ezio's gaze was locked on him now, clear, unwavering.

"Forget those bastards at the base. The people in that camp? They're coming. To you." Ezio's eyes bored into Kev. "Count on it."

Kev swallowed. In the back, the others groggily murmured their agreement.

Ezio turned in his seat, toward Kev. "No matter what you hear on that radio—turn it off if you have to. Hold on to that picture of your family and stay. You stay, and you save these people. Got it?"

Kev's grip firmed on the wheel. "Yes, Cap."

Ezio held out a fist. "You're one of us now." The edge in his voice eased, but the steel stayed. "We never run. We never leave anyone behind."

Glasgow, Present Day
Queen Elizabeth University Hospital Car Park – Night

Gina and Annabelle moved through the hospital reception, their shoes slapping softly yet audibly against the polished floor.

The lone security guard looked up, blinking at the unexpected sight. Before he could find his voice, they were on him, smiles sharp, voices smooth, toying with him, keeping his focus where they wanted it.

Behind them, Ezio, Reddy and Chris slipped through the entrance, dressed in black, duffel bags slung low. They moved fast, straight for the elevator.

Gina's tone shifted. Accusing now. Eyes cold. "What did you just say?" She snatched at the guard's badge, voice rising. "Give me your name."

The guard stumbled over his own words, hands up, defensive. His face burned red as they spun on their heels, leaving him floundering.

He turned back to his computer, exhaling. Didn't notice Gina slide his pass across the floor, nudging it with her foot.

Ezio stopped it with his boot.

Morocco, One Year Earlier
Desert, Near Tangier – Night

Kev stood alone. Glancing at his watch, he shifted on his feet. Fire and explosions lit up the night, smoke billowing across the sky. Overhead, rotor blades thundered, cutting through the chaos. He spun, tracking the lights banking away, streaking back toward base.

Figures moved on the horizon, small, distant. Moving toward him.

"They did it," he murmured.

His radio squawked, yanking him back.

"Corporal, come in!"

Kev scrambled into the driver's seat, grabbed the transmitter. "O'Connell here! They did it!"

"Corporal, the mission's a bust. Return to base, hostiles inbound!"

"No," Kev snapped. "It's not hostiles. He got them out. Ezio told me to wait."

Static. Then a voice—tense, fraying at the edges. "The package—shit's sake, O'Connel, it's not what we thought. The Wolves lost their CIA asset. She's fucking dead, mate. You need to move. Now."

Kev's whole body tensed. He stared through the windscreen, jaw tight. "He told me you'd say that."

"Blast it, Corporal! It's fucked, it's all fucked!"

Kev shut off the radio. Focused on the figures moving closer.

"I won't let you down, Captain."

A high-pitched whine split the night. The RPG streaked past, missing by inches. Kev barely had time to curse before the ground erupted, the shockwave sending him diving headfirst back into his Humvee.

Glasgow, Present Day
Queen Elizabeth University Hospital Car Park – Night

The group huddled around the car, Kev's voice clear through the speakers.

Annabelle froze, stalled mid-air, clutching a closed comms radio. A glance at

Marty, Jock, Gina, Skip. The unease was spreading, thickening between them.

Marty caught it first. "What?"

"Lost their asset?" The words barely made it out. "That's not—" She hesitated. "Ezio, that's not how you told it."

Her fingers curled around the radio, white-knuckled. She swallowed hard. "It went wrong, didn't it?"

Glasgow, Present Day
Queen Elizabeth University Hospital
Express Elevator – Night

Ezio stood still, head low, eyes on the horizon.

Reddy adjusted his radio. "Annie, just… leave it. Please."

A pause. Then Annabelle, uncertain, "But, I thought…"

Chris exhaled. "It didn't go how we told you." He glanced at Ezio, but Ezio said nothing, staring past them, past the edge of the rooftop to the night sky.

The radio crackled. Annabelle's voice again, smaller this time. "Was it… Inaya?"

Chris met Ezio's hollow stare. His nod was slight, but it landed heavy.

"Yeah. Inaya."

Glasgow, Present Day
Queen Elizabeth University Hospital Car Park - Night

Annabelle watched Marty. His face creased in regret as he thought about his earlier outburst at Ezio.

Nobody spoke.

Gina folded her arms. Jock exhaled, shaking his head. A quiet horror crept among them.

Morocco, One Year Earlier
Inside a Known Terrorist Compound Near Tangier – Night

Earlier, Ezio had described it to Kev in fragments— dust, heat, loss. Now, Kev unknowingly spoke it back through his hacked mobile mic. The memory played out again, raw and undiluted. This time, for all to hear.

The air reeked of burning fuel, thick and bitter, but Ezio barely noticed. The heat, the dust, the gunfire—it all blurred into the chaos hammering through his skull. He pushed forward, shaking off Reddy's grip, ignoring Chris's pull at his arm.

"Inaya!" His voice ripped through the night, ragged, desperate.

She was there, sprawled on the floor. She was trapped, bleeding out. Firelight danced across her face—still, beautiful, even now. Her deep blue eyes locked onto his, glassy with pain.

Chris yanked at him. "Ezio, you're gonna get yourself killed!"

"I don't care!" His voice cracked. He strained, gaining a forward step. "She's pregnant! I love her, our fucking child!"

Reddy and Chris faltered, the fight in their grip easing just enough. Ezio lurched forward, reaching—closer now.

"Inaya, stay with me!"

Her lips moved as she whispered something he couldn't hear over the roar of the chopper, the gunfire splitting the night. Then her head tipped sideways. The light in her eyes dimmed.

Ezio dropped to his knees. Heat licked at his skin, but he didn't feel it. He reached out, fingers trembling, useless.

"No."

A scream tore through him, raw, hopeless.

Reddy hauled him back, his grip monstrous. "She's gone! There's nothing you can do!"

Ezio strained, ready to swing, to fight. His fists curled, but the strength wasn't there. His chest heaved, the breath ripped from him in broken gasps.

Chris gritted his teeth and hauled him up. "Sorry, mate. We've got to go."

His legs buckled. Reddy and Chris didn't let him fall. They dragged him toward the extraction point…

Glasgow, Present Day
Queen Elizabeth University Hospital – Night

Annabelle covered her mouth, breath unsteady. She blinked fast, swallowed it down.

Marty shifted, almost reached for her, then thought better of it. His fingers brushed hers as he eased the radio from her grip. He hesitated, then clicked the button. "Look, when I said earlier…" His voice caught.

Upstairs, Ezio and the Wolves moved fast. Hospital corridors, double doors, the helideck ramp ahead. The hum of rotor blades in the distance. Ezio walked with his head low, exhaled through his nose. A brief smile, almost embarrassed. "Hey," he murmured. "Don't worry about it. We get him out. We don't leave anyone behind."

The Wolves spread out under the helideck. The expected thump of helicopter rotor blades grew louder. Steady. Unstoppable.

Reddy grinned. "And we sure as hell don't run."

Annabelle climbed into the passenger seat, the radio firm in her grip. Marty buckled in, Jock in the back, quiet, bracing.

Annabelle pressed the mic. "Except into a fight."

Chris snorted, shot a look at Reddy. "Well. Not exactly." He checked himself, considered. "But this time? Maybe we do."

Already on the move, Skip steered onto the motorway. Gina listened in, radio in hand, her smirk slight. Approval in it. She keyed the mic, voice smooth, controlled.

"We're moving. I'll be set up before you get there."

Ezio's voice came back, rough but steady. "Thanks. For having my back."

Gina didn't answer. Just watched the road. Eyes fixed. Fire in them now.

Chapter 7

Glasgow, Present Day
Old Church Cardross – Night

Eammon stared at Kev, a smirk of ridicule tugging at his mouth. Across from him, Alexei Semenov leaned back, arms folded. Unimpressed.

"Boring," Alexei scoffed. His voice bounced off the stone walls.

Eammon didn't look at him. Eyes on Kev. "And in case you haven't noticed," he said, "you are very much left behind."

Kev grinned through defiant eyes. "That's what you think."

Semenov barked. Eammon snorted. The men around them followed, the sound of laughter rolling through the room.

Eammon let his gaze drift over Kev. The missing shoes. The ropes. He shook his head. "You're alone. No shoes. I don't know why you have no shoes. It's ridiculous, but how exactly are you not left behind?"

Alexei smirked. "It's so he can't run."

Eammon cut him a look, barely concealing contempt. "That won't." He waved the idea away, then turned back to Kev. "Where's the package?"

Kev's eyes widened. "You mean the guns?"

Eammon's hissed. "Of course not!"

Alexei cackled. He couldn't help himself. "You fool, I'm after a big bloody bag of diamonds."

Kev laughed. A real laugh. "Oh, I know," he said.

Eammon frowned. The men around him shifted, uncertain.

Glasgow, Present Day
A898 – Night

Annabelle's hand found Marty's free one, a quiet pressure as his other gripped the wheel, knuckles white. Kev's voice came steady through the radio.

"I know," Kev said, condescending as hell.

Eammon came back, voice tight with fury. "Yeah, well, so did Morris. That's why Marty was here. You got played, mate.

Morris is finished. He stopped the syndicate heroin, shut it down. But those diamonds? They'll buy it back. You could've made double. But now?" He laughed, a dry, hollow thing. "You're all dead."

Kev answered without hesitation. "The story's not over yet."

Eammon sighed, a long-suffering exhale. "Really?"

Silence inside the SUV. Marty's grip tightened on the wheel. He shot Jock a sharp, questioning look. Jock shifted, gaze darting to the window, restless.

"Oh, don't give me that," Jock muttered. "What about the diamonds, eh?"

Marty checked the rear-view mirror, locking eyes with Jock. A slow breath leaving him. "We all have to look out for our own."

Annabelle scoffed, half bitter, half amused. "Yeah. You've got Parker. We've got each other."

Marty nodded. Thought about that. "Yeah," he said, glancing at her. She squeezed his hand, understanding. He picked up the radio.

"I'm gonna say, lads… at this point, it does sound like you've left him."

A pause.

Then Reddy's voice, smug. "You might think that. But then I saved the day."

Chris came through, dry as ever. "You?"

Reddy huffed. "It was my brilliant idea."

Glasgow, Present Day
Queen Elizabeth University Hospital Heli-Deck – Night

Under the whir of rotors and strobing lights, Chris chuckled, shaking his head as the Wolves waited for a patient to be wheeled past. He and Reddy worked fast, securing their gear at the edge of the helipad, staying out of sight as the hospital crew moved inside.

"You've got to give him that," Ezio said.

Chris raised his voice over the thudding blades. "It was crazy and terrifying," he shouted, shooting Reddy an approving nod. "But brilliant."

Reddy grinned, puffing up. Ezio smirked. "And what, this is normal?"

Chris laughed. "More normal than that was."

Reddy shrugged, unbothered.

The last of the hospital crew disappeared inside. Ezio lifted his chin. "Alright. Let's go again."

The Wolves moved as one, swift and soundless, gliding up the ramp. On the helideck, the noise covered their approach. They fanned out, weapons raised, shadowed figures closing in on the cockpit.

Morocco, One Year Earlier
Ben Guerir Air Base – Night

The Black Hawks touched down in the dark, rotors tearing up dust. Boots hit the ground. Ezio jumped out first, shoving the detainee ahead of him. Chris and Reddy flanked him, wired tight. Ezio's face was streaked, dust and sweat clinging to the tracks of tears. He held himself together by sheer force of will, anger and grief balanced on a knife's edge.

"Thanks for the lift," Ezio called back.

The American pilot nodded. "Anytime, Haggis. We're all sorry for your loss, man."

Ezio clenched his jaw, pushed the detainee forward. The pilot turned to his radio. His face darkened.

"Haggis, your convoy's taking fire. Casualties. Bad. Real bad. You need to get them out."

Ezio spun. "Take us back."

"Not happening, brother. Orders came in. Priority list, and you're not on it anymore. We've got U.S. troops to pull from the shit up north."

Reddy caught Ezio by the shoulder, voice low. "Cap, you're not okay."

"I'm fine," Ezio snapped. "We just… we need to go back."

The pilot tipped his head towards a British officer waiting nearby, ready to receive the detainee from Chris. Smug bastard. "Your boy's got birds, doesn't he?"

Ezio turned, eyes locking on the officer. He jerked his chin to Reddy. Reddy grinned and jogged off. Ezio stayed put.

The officer scowled, shaking his head before Ezio even opened his mouth. "No troop carriers."

Ezio's voice cut sharp. "I told him to stay. Because of me."

"Not a shock," the officer muttered.

Ezio stepped closer. "What's that supposed to mean?"

Chris knew the tone. A warning, sharp as a blade.

The officer took his time looking Ezio up and down, sheer contempt leaking from every pore. He sneered. "You, Captain," he hissed, "fancy yourself a legend. When in fact you are nothing more than a little gobby, sloppy, brutish Jock. Someone I would ordinarily tolerate, but your overly aggressive tendencies continue to compromise the operation!"

Ezio hit him before he could smirk. One sharp, clean shot. The officer's face hit the tarmac, blood smearing his chin. He squirmed, gasping.

Ezio barely spared him a look. "I *am* the operation." He walked off.

Reddy reappeared, grinning like a lunatic. "Capo," he said, eyes gleaming. "You're gonna love this."

Ezio and Chris slowed.

"We've got Apaches," Reddy said, arms wide like he was announcing Christmas morning.

Chris exhaled. He looked at Ezio.

"Ah, fuck it," he said. "Why not?"

Glasgow, Present Day
Pollock Country Park – Night

Pollok Country Park lay quiet under the grey Glasgow sky, the manicured lawns slick with earlier rain, leaves clung to stone pathways. Beyond the trees, Pollok House stood in shadow, a grand estate that had seen better days.

Morris sat on a wrought-iron bench near the old walled garden, shoulders easy. Joe sat next to him, stiff as rebar. From a distance, they looked like two old friends taking the air.

"So," Morris said, "this is how you're going to play it? You were my buffer, now you want to be a barrier?"

Joe stared at the gravel. "It's what they want," he muttered. "You've become the opposite of what you taught me. You're in the way."

Morris gazed out across the wide stretch of lawn, the paths winding off into the trees. "Strange, isn't it? We're in one of the cleanest parts of the city. You can almost believe nothing rotten ever happens here."

Joe shifted, unsure where this was going.

"Progress, is it?" Morris turned to him. "That what they're selling you now?"

"You always told me to keep moving forward. Not to stagnate."

"Heroin's not progress, Joe. Not in this city. I won't be the man who poisons what I built."

Morris leaned in. "Unfortunately for you, the reason you can't see that… is because I made you exactly what I needed."

Joe squirmed on the rain-soaked bench, arse damp, the smell of Morris's aftershave thick from his coat. He felt the man's breath at his neck.

"What?"

"We're both exactly where we're meant to be," said Morris.

Joe inhaled, too late. "What could an old…"

Morris's fist caught him clean on the chin. Before Joe could react, the knife slipped from Morris's sleeve and sank into his temple. Joe's eyes went wide. Blood ran down his face, tracked his cheek as he slumped sideways, dead weight against the iron armrest.

Morris quickly pulled Joe's phone from his pocket, swiping. The lock screen flashed as he bypassed it with ease.

Screen lock deactivated. Set new lock code.

Morris scrolled to the recent calls and dialled straight to the syndicate.

Glasgow, Present Day
Cardross Roadside – Night

Gina's SUV slid to a stop beside Marty's, gravel spitting under the tyres. The outline of the old church silhouetted against the moonlit sky ahead of them. She rolled down her window, stuck two fingers up at him. "The package?"

Marty scowled. "You've been listening the whole time, and that's your first concern?"

Gina leaned out slightly. "My first concern is my father's empire hanging by a thread. Second is that package. Where is it?"

Marty ground his teeth. "Still inside."

"Useless…" she muttered. Then snapped, "It's secure?"

"Clearly," he snapped back. "One would think that's why a squad of Semenov's lot are holed up in there, wouldn't you?"

She snorted. "Whatever. I'll be on the ridge." She pointed a sharp finger at him. "Stick to the plan."

"Skip!" she barked. Then she was gone, the SUV whipped away into the night, tyres kicking up dust, leaving Marty glowering at fading tail lights.

Glasgow, Present Day
Queen Elizabeth University Hospital Heli-Deck – Night

Reddy stood outside the helicopter, rifle raised. Inside, Chris had his own weapon trained on the pilots. Out of the shadows, Ezio stepped forward, the cockpit's glow catching his face. Calm. That faint, wry smile.

"Good evening."

Jonesy's face lit up. "Capo!"

Ezio grinned. "Hi, Jonesy."

The co-pilot, younger, too eager, nudged his colleague. "This the Wolf?"

"Not now, Tom," she muttered, eyes back on Ezio. "You boys still on the job?"

Ezio's grin widened slightly. Chris lowered his rifle, pulled two thick wads of cash from his jacket, and passed them over. Jonesy's brows lifted. Tom looked ready to combust.

Ezio leaned into the cockpit, all charm. "Domestic terrorism," he said, continuing casually as if exchanging office gossip over a bistro coffee. "Need-to-know basis. But here's something for your troubles, hush money." He tossed the cash onto the console. "We all love hush money, am I right?"

Tom's jaw dropped. "That's got to be a hundred grand," he squeaked.

"Fifty each." Ezio shrugged. "What's your salary again? Never mind." He tapped the stack of cash with a finger. "You could even buy me that pint. I'll give you a discount at Mullholland."

Jonesy and Tom exchanged a glance. It took seconds.

Jonesy tucked her share away, resting a hand on the controls. "Welcome aboard, Captain." A wink.

Ezio's grin was quick. He motioned Reddy inside. The big man ambled into the cabin and crouched on the floor, unfolding a map. Chris joined him. The others followed, closing in.

Ezio nodded, eyes sharp. "Right. Here's what I need from you…"

The helicopter lifted from the helipad, Glasgow spilling out beneath them, a glittering sprawl. The River Clyde snaked black through the lights. The rotors thumped steady, filling the cabin. A sound that once carried over a different, far less forgiving place.

Morocco, One Year Earlier
Desert Sky – Night

Against the darkened sky, two Apache attack helicopter silhouettes moved through the air, their profiles as unmistakable as they were menacing.

"Alpha Sixteen, you are ordered to turn back. This is an unauthorised use of British assets…"

The radio transmission died mid-sentence.

Ezio hung off the lead helicopter's wing, wind whipping at him, the wolf insignia on his shoulder worn and fierce. Behind him, Reddy and Chris clung to the second Apache.

On the ground, chaos spread, swift and uncontainable, rippling outward like wildfire. Kev's overturned Humvee marked the end of the shattered convoy, survivors scrambling, caught between the muzzle flashes.

Jonesy's voice broke through closed comms, steady, crisp.

"Capo, Wolves. Compound in range. Aggressive infiltration and fire suppression in thirty seconds."

Inside the wrecked Humvee, Kev fought his seatbelt, breath jagged, fuel dripping onto his face, sand clinging where it shouldn't. Bullets slammed into steel.

Boots. Close now.

Kev clenched his jaw, braced.

Then the sky erupted. Rotors. Cannon fire. The world shaking under the weight of it.

"Dismount."

Ezio unlatched his harness, rolled off the Apache's wing. Chris and Reddy hit the sand. The Wolves fanned out, sweeping forward gunfire ripping through the night.

Ezio reached the wreckage. The blade flashed, Kev's scream caught in his throat as the belt tore free.

"Move."

Kev staggered to his feet, propelled forward by Ezio's grip. The Marines fell back in sync, the four of them sprinting away from the Humvee. Just as they cleared it, a thunderous explosion rocked the night, flames erupting from the wreckage, searing against the cool desert air, the shockwave hurling the four across the sand.

Glasgow, Present Day
Above the River Clyde – Night

The helicopter tore through the night, the Clyde a black ribbon beneath them. Rotors pounded, their rhythm pulling past and present into the same relentless beat.

Chris checked the FRIES rig, giving the ropes one last tug. "Good thing we brought the real deal," he muttered.

Reddy glanced out the window, then back. "Aye, didn't think I'd be doing this when I woke up." He cracked his neck.

"Mind you, had a belter of a hangover. Wasn't thinking much at all." He nodded at Ezio. "Bit of fresh air does a body good, eh, Cap?"

Ezio glanced up, smirked. Chris cut in before he could answer, tapping Reddy's wrist piece. "Way past your bedtime now, big man."

Reddy checked his watch, rumbled out a laugh. He pushed up to full height, spreading his arms so Chris had to duck aside. Cleared his throat.

"It is dawn. The earth stirs. The long night soon breaks, and with it, we rise! Grateful that we might chance to fight the same battles with new strength."

Chris and Ezio exchanged looks. Even Jonesy and Tom turned from the cockpit, eyebrows raised.

Reddy wasn't done.

"Once more unto the breach, dear friends, once more! Courage and fear walk hand in hand, for the dawn is fucking Reddy's to command!"

Silence.

Then his laughter erupted, deep and rolling, and the rest caught it, the cabin shaking with it as the helicopter closed in on its target.

Glasgow, Present Day
Old Church Cardross – Dawn

Eammon rose from his haunches, pulled his pistol, and aimed it at Kev's forehead. He cast a glance at Alexei, muttered under his breath. "Enough. He's stalling." His face hardened. Almost sorrowful. "Sorry, mate. We're leaving. You're not." He cocked the gun.

The church fell silent. Kev swallowed.

Then, something. A low hum, barely there at first, growing like a tremor through the stone walls. Eammon faltered. His grip slackened. He looked to Semenov. Confusion turned to dread.

"Nah…" He barely breathed it.

A red dot blinked onto Semenov's forehead. His skull exploded.

Blood and bone sprayed across Eammon. He stumbled, blinking, breath catching in his throat. Alexei Semenov lay headless at his feet.

Up on the ridge, Gina sighed. Lowered her rifle. She switched off the laser sight, exhaled through her nose, and slipped back into the SUV. "Go," she said.

Skip floored it. Tyres screeching as they tore down the hill, stopping sharp beside Marty's car.

Inside, no one moved. No one breathed. Semenov's men stood frozen, eyes wide, hands slack at their sides.

Above, the thudding *chop, chop, chop* of helicopter blades.

Gina stepped out, caught the MP5 Skip tossed her from the weapons cache. Checked the safety, nodded to Marty. He returned it, twenty paces away. On the far side, Annabelle raised a hand. When she was sure they were watching, she dropped it.

They moved together, spreading wide, emptying their magazines into the stone walls in short, precise bursts.

Inside, all hell broke loose.

Windows shattered, the lights went out, glass rained down. Flashbangs detonated, hammering light into the corners of the church. Semenov's men scrambled, crashing over pews, scattering into blind panic as gunfire ripped into the wood and stone around them.

Outside, at the rear of the church, Jock grinned, flipping the cover shut on the church's electrical panel.

Three figures descended from above, fast-roping through the broken windows.

Chris hit the ground first, sprinted for Kev. Reddy and Ezio moved in behind him, weapons raised, cutting through the chaos with sharp bursts of gunfire, slamming stocks into ribs, boots into knees. No wasted movement.

Three beeps.

The lights came on.

Marty stormed through the front doors. Gina darted past him, arriving just in time to catch a thug aiming at Ezio. Without hesitation dropped the man mid-step before he could even turn on Ezio. Her shot cracked through the open space.

Chris worked the straps on Kev's wrists. Jock wrestled the ones at his ankles.

Ezio and Reddy kept moving, dropping the last resistance, clearing a path.

Then—Marty's gasp.

Eammon. Disoriented, raising a gun.

Ezio turned, caught a blow to the jaw before he could react.

Marty didn't think. Just moved.

"No!" He crashed into Eammon, sent them both sprawling. The shot went wide.

They hit the floor, grappling for control of the gun.

Then—a gasp. Gina staggered.

A red bloom spread across her side.

Eammon grinned. "Part of your plan?"

Marty's grip tightened. He wrenched free, slammed down on Eammon's wrist. A crack. A scream. The gun jerked toward Eammon's throat. Marty pulled the trigger.

Blood sprayed across Marty's face as Eammon's body went slack.

Silence.

Annabelle was already there, hands on Marty. Checking him. Steadying him, pulling him close. Thanking her lucky stars.

Ezio and Reddy cleared the last of them. A sharp crack—Ezio snapped the arm of the one who'd landed a punch, let him drop. The man groaned, curled in on himself.

Then, nothing.

Ezio wiped blood from his mouth. Looked around. No more threats. No more movement.

Then Gina spoke.

"Oh?" she muttered, frowning as she touched her side, as if confused to find blood soaking through her shirt.

Heads turned.

Chris cut the last of Kev's bindings. Kev staggered upright, dazed. Reddy stepped forward. Ezio was already moving.

For a second, he just stared. At the blood, the way Gina's knees gave out, how she sank like the floor had been pulled from her.

And something in him buckled too.

He didn't shout. Didn't break. But inside, he split open.

He'd been here before. A woman bleeding out in front of him. A wound he hadn't seen coming. A body going cold. Not Gina, not her.

Ezio hit the ground hard beside her, skidding to his knees. Pressed his hands to the wound, fast and firm. He was shaking.

"Stay with me," he barked. "You're alright."

Reddy dropped beside him, calm, focused as he assessed the damage. "Pressure. Keep it there."

Annabelle hauled Marty upright. He groaned, his weight on her. Skip jogged in, slid under Marty's other arm.

Chris checked the injury. His face said it all. "She needs a hospital."

Annabelle shook her head. "A shootout like this? We walk in with that, we're all getting nicked."

Gina let out a breathless, almost amused laugh. "Oh well, in that case, don't fuss."

Marty barely looked at her. "Hardly. She's Morris Kingston's daughter. That bastard could shut down a hospital wing, order room service and no one would have the balls to question it."

He wiped blood from his face and glanced back at her, softer now.

"She'll be fine."

But Ezio wasn't listening. His hands stayed tight, like letting go meant she'd vanish.

Like someone else whom he'd never see again.

Glasgow, Present Day
Old Church Cardross – Morning

Jonesy gave a lazy wave through the cockpit window as the helicopter lifted, rolling through the mist. Inside, Gina leaned against the glass, watching the ground slip away. Skip sat beside her, delivered a quiet nod to the figures below.

Ezio stood still, eyes tracking the ascent. Reddy and Chris flanked him, squared shoulders, steady. Marty strode in from under the rotor wash, glancing back once at the creeping sunrise.

"That was one hell of a night, lads," said Marty.

Reddy clapped a heavy hand on Ezio's shoulder. "We've had worse."

Chris snorted. "So… home time?"

Ezio nodded, lips twitching toward a smile. "Aye. Home time."

As they turned, Annabelle shot past, moving fast. A blur of purpose. She slammed into Marty, grabbed his hand, dragged him toward the SUV without so much as a word. He flushed, hesitated—then let her.

The Wolves chuckled, watching.

Chris leaned back, called out. "Coming with us, then?"

Marty, already being hauled into the car, gave a sheepish grin. Jock held the door open, ushering them in before climbing behind the wheel.

Reddy, true to form, drove an elbow into Chris's ribs and took off at a sprint for the driver's seat of his own vehicle. Chris staggered, straightened, and shot Ezio a look.

Ezio shrugged. "You wouldn't trade him for the world, though. Would you?"

Chris stretched, wincing. "Maybe for a cold beer and a warm woman."

Ezio laughed, climbed into the back of their four-by-four, and finally—finally—closed his eyes.

EPILOGUE

Glasgow, the Following Evening
Mullholland Bar – Night

The bar glowed in amber light, warm against polished wood and glinting glass. Kate McCabe played the piano, fingers drifting over the keys, a half-empty glass of white wine at her side. A soft tune that settled into the bones, familiar as home.

Marty and Annabelle sat close. Her hand rested on his arm, light but firm, as if letting go wasn't an option.

Across the room, Ezio, Chris, and Reddy nursed a bottle of Macallan. The whisky caught the light as they clinked glasses. Laughter cut through the low murmur of conversation, the usual weight on their shoulders giving way to something rare. Easy.

Chiara and Jock laced between tables, laying down fresh rounds.

Kev leaned against the piano, watching. He took a drink from Jock without looking, phone in hand, something glinting in his eye. He wandered over to the table, turning the screen toward Annabelle and Marty.

They glanced at it and laughter spilled from them, unguarded and easy.

Morocco, One Year Earlier
Ben Guerir Air Base – Night

Kev, battered and bloodied, lay on the stretcher, barely holding himself steady as they lifted him from the MEDEVAC Humvee. Ezio, just as bruised, grinned through exhaustion and jumped down, falling into step beside him.

"Found your phone, by the way." Ezio crouched, fishing it from his pocket. He raised it, snapped a quick selfie—both of them grinning like idiots. Hard-earned relief in every line of their dirt-streaked faces— Kev slumped in torn, fire-singed U.S fatigues, Ezio calm beside him, Royal Marine kit faded, unmarked by rank or official regiment, fashionably dusted with desert sand. The kind of look worn by men who don't officially exist.

Glasgow, Present
Mullholland Bar – Night

Kev chuckled, passing his phone around. The old photo sparked a string of laughter, Chiara held it for a lingering moment, smiling warmly before handing it off. One by one, they leaned in to see, their smiles growing wider.

A knock at the door took the edge off the laughter. Nobody rushed to answer.

Reddy groaned, pushing himself up from his seat. He shuffled his way to the door, muttering under his breath, and swung it open.

Morris Kingston stood before him, rainwater streaming off him, his coat hanging heavy. The room quieted. Reddy glanced back at Ezio.

Ezio took a moment, staring at Morris. Then, with difficulty, he resigned himself to giving the faintest nod of consent.

Reddy stepped aside.

Morris walked in and the bar hushed, all eyes turning to him as the imposing gangster swept his eyes across the room, landing on Marty.

Marty's grin faded into something more cautious.

But Morris just looked at him steadily, almost understanding. He pulled up a chair beside Ezio, the wood scraping harshly against the floor.

Ezio studied Morris, then looked around the room, at his people. His family. Reddy set an empty whisky glass between them. Ezio smiled wistfully at the glass and, to the relief of the room, poured a small amount from his bottle. He pushed the glass across the woodgrain of the table toward Morris. Neither man looked at the other, but the acknowledgment was there. Appreciated.

"Heard you had a rough night," Morris said, eyes on the glass.

Ezio snorted. "Heard you had a shift yourself."

Morris gave a dry chuckle, exhaled slowly. He rubbed at his neck, eyes distant. "Had to send a message."

His stubby fingers traced the rim of the glass before he finally looked at Ezio. For once, honest. "They'll be coming for us now. All of us."

Ezio held his stare, confident. "Let them." He looked around the room at the people who mattered—the ones who would stand by his side when it counted, their fierce loyalty reflected back to him. He lifted his glass.

Morris clinked his in response, a shadow of a smile breaking the stone of his stoic old face.

Reddy, grinning, shot to his feet, raising his drink high. "Let's get pissed!"

Laughter cracked around the room. Tension evaporating, glasses clinked, voices lifting in a rough, joyful chorus.

As the laughter simmered, Marty's attention drifted back to Annabelle for a moment. Taking her in. He looked from Annabelle to Morris with pity. "Gina?" Marty asked.

Morris gave Marty that old wry smile. "She's fine, she might be proudly sporting a little badge of honour the next time she is flaunting herself on the beach, but she's receiving the best care money can buy. Rest will do her good, son. I'd be more worried about poor old Skip. I've put that bloody toerag under strict orders not to leave her side."

Marty shook his head. "They'll drive each other crazy," he said.

Then fished in his pocket.

Marty pulled out a small velvet pouch, setting it on the table between himself, Ezio, and Morris. The room stilled once again, more so this time as heads turned to that pouch— everyone knew what it was. What it meant.

Morris looked up from the pouch to meet Marty's hard stare. Regret flashed, quick and fleeting, before he looked down again.

He rasped, resignation. "It'll split nicely."

Marty's mouth curled into a wry smile. The room took its cue, tension giving way to the hum of quiet acceptance.

Ezio watched them both, then let his focus drift, felt his aching body ease as drinking and laughter rolled back through the room.

Ezio

We left our old lives in the shadows, chasing certainty, hoping to be the heroes of our own story.

But the truth?

There's no black and white.

We live in the grey. We've always lived in the grey.

The shadows belong to us, ours to move within, on our terms.

And we're just getting started.

About the Author

Chris Black is an ROV Supervisor, operating subsea robotic systems primarily in the North Sea. At home in Dalgety Bay, Fife, he serves under the rule of three very opinionated cats. Alongside his wife Angie, Chris spends his rare spare time attempting overly ambitious furniture builds for their feline overlords. If you're ever looking for a conversation you might not escape, just mention cats.

Chris has played the lead in several independent feature films and also has experience in voiceover and short-form storytelling.

Capo is his first novel and part of a broader creative vision he's actively developing as a feature film. The story doesn't end here, he's already at work on the sequel. Keep an eye out for the return of Ezio and his Wolves.

Connect with Chris at:

www.blackartsdevelopment.com

Reached the end of Capo and purchased the special edition bundle?
Now's the time to open your Top Secret envelope and uncover the classified files—safe to do now that you've finished the story.

Curious about those secrets or want to grab your own special edition bundle? Head to:

www.blackartsdevelopment.com

Enjoyed the book?
A quick review on Goodreads or Amazon goes a long way in helping others discover the story.

Thank you for reading

CAPO

Printed in Dunstable, United Kingdom